Sea Song de le Corsaire

LOVE SONGS FROM DEUS

Sea Song
de le Corsaire

4 Horsemen
Publications, Inc.

LYRA R. SAENZ

Table of Contents

Dedication

To Hans Christian Andersen and all
the lost lovers of the past who were denied their happy
endings by a world too cruel to have them.

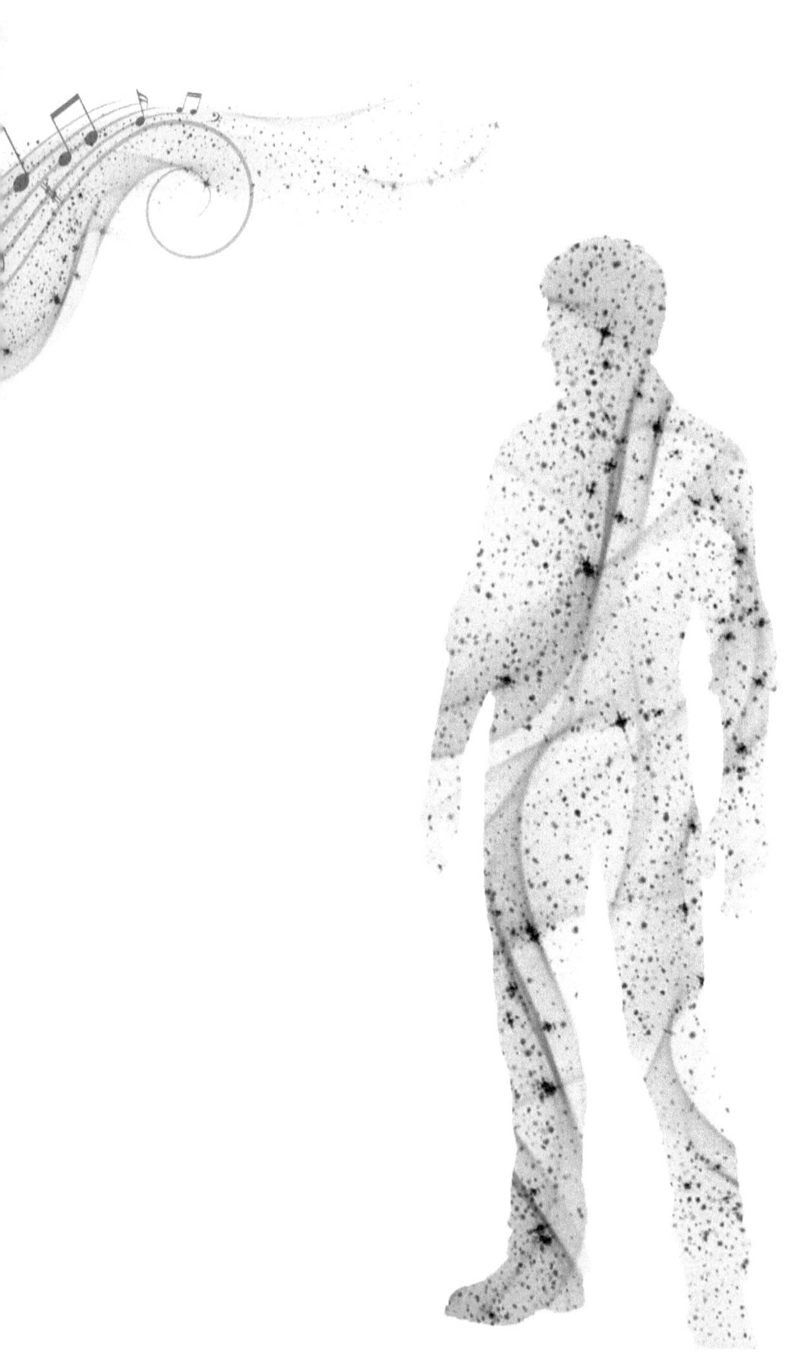

Prologue

My clothes are all in pawn
Go down you blood red roses, go down
And it's mighty draughty around Cape Horn
Go down you blood red roses, go down
Oh, you pinks and posies
Go down you blood red roses, go down

It's round Cape Horn we've got to go
Chasing whales through ice and snow

Oh, my old mother she wrote to me
My darling son come home from sea

Oh, it's one more pull and that will do
For we're the bullies to kick her through

"Blood Red Roses"
An Old World Sea Shanty

LEON HAD ALWAYS LOVED THE SEA. Growing up to a fisherman father and fishwife mother, it was easy to understand why.

He learned to swim before he could walk, he learned to write in the beach sand, and he learned his numbers counting seashells on his father's fishing boat. His mother used to call him a fish out of water whenever he would toddle across the beach to dive headfirst into the surf. She used to joke that were it not for the nine months she carried him in her womb, she would think his father found him on a fishing voyage. His father used to praise him, saying a fisherman needed to love the ocean because the sea goddess would care for him so long as he too cared for her.

So, yes, Leon loved the sea.

He loved to dive into its depths and explore the seabed. He loved the colorful coral reefs, living paintings unlike anything ever seen on land. He loved the magnificence of watching a whale or shark breach. He loved swimming alongside seals and otters as they rode the waves to shore. He loved the calm rocking of a boat under his feet and watching the reflection of the moons dancing over the glassy surface.

He even loved the less gentle, more turbulent aspects of the ocean. He loved the way the storms made the water crash and roll—how the ocean never held back in its rage. He loved the blatant juxtaposition between life and death that a life at sea exemplified.

But most of all, he loved how, when he was lonely or sad, lost or afraid, or sometimes even just tired, he could pretend, for just a little bit, that the sea was singing to him.

Blow the Man Down

Fifteen men on the dead man's chest—
...Yo-ho-ho, and a bottle of rum!
Drink and the devil had done for the rest—
...Yo-ho-ho, and a bottle of rum!
An old world sea shanty from Treasure Island
By Robert Louis Stevenson

12th Day in the Month of Storms—1825 A.P.

"LEON, DO YOU MIND FINISHING THIS, mate? I've gotta piss."

Izacc all but throws the line Leon's way, and the twenty-one-year-old has to scramble to keep the spell cannon from rolling across the deck as the old, raggedy lycan stalks off with a wolfish laugh without tying the damn thing down. Leon grunts as the full weight of it nails him in his mechanical shoulder.

"Izacc, you bastard! You can't just leave a cannon loose!" shouts Leon as he finishes tying it off, careful not to smear the sigils etched across its body. The rope pulls taut, and he flexes his fingers, organic bone and muscle jointed with bolts and framed in steel. He straightens to standing and sighs as his upper back cracks, tilting his head sideways until another satisfying crack sounds as the hooks and cables that comprise his exoskeleton realign with fleshy vertebral ligaments. The release of tension is so good he feels it all the way to his toes. "Why do we even still have cannons anyway when we have a fucking LDS?"

"The Laser Defense System doesn't replace a need for fire power." Yoshi, their resident witch, comes to help him finish tying off the weapon.

"So, I say we replace these ancient hunks of garbage with a machine gun."

"I can't fire magic at technomancers with a machine gun, Leon." The witch winks his blue eye at Leon, the other a milky, unseeing white. Yoshi unloads a basket of glowing silver spheres, the witch's latest haul from the port. Inside each sphere is a spell locked in stasis. Once set off by the spell cannon, any number of effects will activate, from fireballs to lightning strikes.

"Not sure the trade-off is worth it."

He'll be lucky if the area doesn't bruise by morning. Next he has the chance, he's going to slug Izacc in the tailbone.

"Aww, is our little mako admitting his pretty augmentations are just for show?"

Yoshi cackles as Leon elbows him in the gut.

"I'll show you just for show," he growls, tackling Yoshi to the deck. The witch goes down in a fit of giggles, and the two wrestle on the ground like a pair of squabbling sea lion pups until a bucket of salt water is poured over both of them.

"Alright, alright, cut it out, you two," chides Cassiopeia. "It's almost sundown, and we've got work to do."

The buxom Amazon of a woman, who acts both as their ship mom and first mate, kicks a bucket at them with her mechanical leg. The bucket flies toward them at what could easily be clocked at 50 mph. While Yoshi flinches away, Leon catches it in both hands.

"I was working," shouts Leon, "until someone decided to throw a cannon at me."

"Oh, you're fine!" calls Izacc, apparently back from pissing with an e-cig between his teeth.

"Yeah," scoffs Leon. "Fine enough to make sure you piss blood for the next week."

He pushes the lycan on the shoulder only to get shoved back. He lunges forward, catching Izacc around the legs. The lycan falls, his upper body shifting from human to wolfish disposition, and a grapple contest unfolds.

"Get 'em, Leon!" shouts Yoshi. "Show him what's what!"

"That's enough, you two."

"Aw, leave 'em be, Cass."

The two devolve into a raucous dogpile of destruction while Yoshi snaps photos of their foolishness. They don't stop until a pistol shot rings from the quarter deck.

"Alright," calls their captain. "That's enough, gents. If we want to get to The Tai Tai by tomorrow, we can't be mucking about."

Guadeloupe Cortez stands looking severe and imposing for all of five seconds before a grin splits his face, and all five of them share a good laugh. How ironic is it that on a ship full of cyborgs and hexen, the human is the one in charge?

"But seriously," says Loupe through his hand, "I just scrubbed that deck, and your sodding bodies are making a mockery of my hard labor. So, get!""

"Aye, aye, captain!" salutes Izacc, no longer wolfed out.

Leon pulls himself onto his feet for a wide bent-knee stretch.

"Leonito, you've got the crow's nest? I want to make sure no one sneaks up on us."

That pinché nickname. As he is about to curse at his captain—

BANG!

The entire ship shudders, and Leon is sent reeling to the floor.

BAM!

The LDS detonates an oncoming missile before it can hit the ship. Flares rain down on their heads. Leon lifts up to peer over the edge of the railing, and sure enough, another vessel is sailing directly toward them.

Military sea dogs.

"We're under attack. Battle stations, Everyone!"

Utter chaos ensues as Leon and his crewmates take to arms. At the helm, Izacc prevents the enemy ship from getting into the boarding zone. It, however, doesn't keep them out of aerial striking range. The enemy crew's drones open fire on the *C-Devil*. They are outgunned three to one, but that doesn't exactly mean much to them. They know how to handle an adept attack.

Kill the operator, not the drone.

Cassiopeia fires on them with a rocket launcher while Loupe works the LDS to take out as much oncoming fire as possible. Izacc and Yoshi work the spell cannons, going back and forth between the three starboard guns as they fire Yoshi's stock of spells. The lycan loads the spheres while Yoshi activates the launch seals and Leon...

Leon is their sharpshooter. His job is to pick off the enemy crew one by one by one with his rifle from the crow's nest.

Leon aims another shot and takes down another adept; his drone goes still, hovering in the air without command. Izacc and Yoshi fire a perfectly aimed spell straight onto the other ship's deck. A tech destabilization fog disrupts the ship's communications, and Leon, ready to fire, takes aim and shoots another sailor down. As he readies another shot, fire floods his senses.

The first shot mangles the robotics on his left arm. The second rips through Leon's flesh, and pain erupts. His vision blackens as he falls backward, out of the nest.

"Leon!"

Leon hears someone shout as he tumbles from the crow's nest. He flips head over heels before landing ass-first in the water. The impact knocks the air out of him, which is probably for the best since he sinks immediately under the surface. His arm is out of commission, white-hot agony as sea salt floods the flesh wound and short circuits the mechanical one. He can still kick, trying to push himself back to the surface, but he's so disoriented, he doesn't know up from down anymore. The sting from the bullet wound burns in the saltwater, and all around him the ocean turns red. His whole body feels numb and cold despite the sun-warmed water around him.

How much blood has he lost?

An explosion goes off next to him, and bullets rain down into the water. One of the shots grazes his already injured shoulder while another one catches his thigh. He dives forward to get out of the line of fire, but as he goes, something wraps around his ankle and yanks.

He immediately thinks "shark," but there is a distinct lack of the pain that comes with flesh being torn apart. *Am I caught on a line?*

He folds himself in half to see if he can find the rope through all of the bubbles obstructing his vision, but his hands don't close over anything material. Whatever is wrapped around him is fleshy, made all the more apparent when the grasp shifts from his ankle to his hands. Something curls itself around his body even as he tries to swim toward the surface, but whatever it is is strong. Strong enough that his kicks don't faze it.

It is as his lungs start to protest the lack of air that he realizes whatever has a hold of him is dragging him deeper into the depths. He gets flashes of the creature, scales and a large burgundy fin, but he also sees tanned skin, glowing orange marks, long black hair, and suddenly, the stories of sailors being lured to their deaths don't seem like fairy tales anymore. Shock manifests as panic, and like a guppy just learning to swim, he inhales seawater, kicking and flailing toward the surface despite the bullets piercing the water. He lashes out at his attacker, but the creature holds firm, dragging him down, down, down until he can no longer see the light of the sun.

This is how he dies. This is how La Santa Muerte comes for him: drowning in the arms of a creature his mother told him stories about. There are red and black scales, webbed hands, the endless blue of the ocean, and not much more as the edges of his vision turn dark. Clawed hands pry his mouth open, soft flesh seals over his lips, and air is pushed into his body.

The flood of oxygen is both a relief and a jolt to his system, and he drinks greedily from the fountain of life-sustaining air. Clawed fingers curl around his head as gentle as a mother cradling her newborn. Abyssal song echoes in his ears, hauntingly beautiful like whalesong. It takes Leon a short eternity to realize what is happening as the fae creature holding him breathes for him. In the throes of the current, Leon drifts, slow and steady and safe, under his savior's guidance even as his limbs leaden with exhaustion and the pressure in his ears makes him dizzy. Between the blood loss and the adrenaline crash, Leon's last bit of strength fails him, and the dark pulls him under.

He allows the gentle rocking of a turbulent sea to carry him off; La Santa Muerte flits away, a specter on the water.

"Leon! Leon!"

The calls of his name are muted as though he has his head ducked under a pool of water, and Leon feels a gentle push set him upward toward those calls.

Leon comes to with a jolt as his head breaks the water's surface. He chokes and sputters and takes in as many lungfuls of fresh air as he can manage. Within a few seconds, two sets of hands are yanking him up and out of the water.

"Leon, pinche vato! You're alive!"

"Brat! You must've saved the emperor or something in a past life to have survived that shitstorm! I don't even fucking know how long you were under."

He is rolled onto his back in the cockboat to Izacc and Yoshi's worried faces. As he is gagging up water, he realizes the sound of cannon and gun fire are absent. He blinks stupidly into the sunlight.

"Yosh? Izacc?"

"They're fine, you bloody guppy."

That at least brings a smile to Leon's face, though he winces when he notices that somewhere between being shot out of the crow's nest and being hauled up by his mates, he's split his lip open as well. How he managed that, he'll never know. Gods below, his head hurts something fierce and his lungs still feel like a fire was lit inside them.

"It's you we all thought were dead. I was afraid I'd be an only child for a second."

Yoshi gives a dramatic faint and fans himself like a swooning woman. It makes Leon laugh at least, even though he is hardly feeling cheery at the moment.

Yeah, Leon thought he was dead, too, when he was dragged into the deep by a... *Wait...*

Leon lurches up from the boat and all but throws his head over the lip and into the water. He opens his eyes and sees nothing but vast fathoms of blue at first, but then he looks toward the deep and sees it, a long shadow flitting by in the darkness. It is large enough to be a shark, but it's the wrong shape and bulk, too sleek, and the tail fin is angled the wrong way, horizontal like mammalian flukes rather than a vertical caudal fin.

He almost dives farther, but Izacc and Yoshi pull him back up.

"Leon! What the hell!"

"Have you lost your damn mind?!"

Leon gapes at the pair.

"I just. I—"

He just what? Wanted to verify that a mermaid just saved his life. Gods, he must be going insane. *Must be the bloodloss.*

"Ahoy, down there! Did you find him?"

"We got 'im, Cassi. He's alright. You can pull us up."

"Fuck." Leon sighs under his breath, reaching up to check his shoulder while Izacc calls up to Cassiopeia that they are ready to be hoisted back up.

"Whoa, whoa, hold up. Let me help you."

Yoshi catches Leon's shoulder and gently pulls back the collar of his tunic to check on the shot. Leon expects the fabric to peel away with a sting, but it just feels wet and maybe a little sticky until the witch freezes entirely.

"What the—"

He looks down to see what Yoshi has paused over. Wrapped around his shoulder is a piece of dark purple seaweed, bound up like a bandage. It's warm to the touch and covered in a thick smelly glaze. Leon reaches up to unravel it. When he drops it to the floor of the boat, it makes a wet, flopping noise. Mysterious seaweed aside, what's more interesting is what Leon has revealed beneath it.

"How in the..." says Yoshi, jaws slack in wonderment.

"I don't know," replies Leon.

He doesn't have a clue how, but the gun wound that had gone through and through on his shoulder is completely healed.

Leon sits up awake that night. It is not a common occurrence, not with his crewmates around him all the time, but tonight... Tonight, in the wake of his near-death experience, he finds no ease in slumber.

It's too quiet, too still for him. It puts his teeth on edge.

You would think loud noises would prove more frightening. Explosions, gunshots, the grind of wood and metal during a crash, thunder during a typhoon, even the rush of water from an oncoming tsunami. These things don't frighten Leon. Loud, while not necessarily good, is predictable. It's the affirmation that the world is still moving around him, and so long as there is motion, Leon can keep slogging his way forward. He can fire his gun at a loud noise, take a stab in the dark with his sword toward rustling movement, or run from the sound of footsteps, if need be, but the quiet? Quiet is unpredictable.

The quiet before and after the noise is the frightening part.

Quiet is the stillness before a calamity. The ocean recedes before the tsunami rises from the depths. The quiet click before a pistol is fired. The quiet comes before the unknown.

And then after...

The silence after the calamity is worse. It is in the quiet when a gunshot victim bleeds out. It is the quiet below the surface of the sea that enfolds sailors as they drown. The total stillness after a crash that prevents movement is what ends life.

He'll never forget how quiet the world became when his father died.

Silence is frightening. Darkness is debilitation. Silent and dark: two words that no doubt describe death.

After today, the last thing Leon wants to feel pressing in on him is the quiet dark.

So, Leon doesn't sleep. He sits instead at the aft of the ship, a stiff blanket wrapped around his shoulders, a lantern at his side as he tinkers with his out-of-whack mechanics. It's a mindless activity, one Leon has carried out hundreds of times before. Maintenance is a daily must for human+, especially after taking a hit like he did today. He'll have to visit his mechanic once they get to Calypso City.

Leon has always loved music. Loved to dance and sing and play the cups when he was a boy. Even after he was indoctrinated into piracy, he still liked to indulge in those pastimes, had a gift for them that made him worth keeping around rather than being tossed overboard or worse by the crew that stole him from his life. He imagines the music now as he sits.

The waves become a tenor, the quiet crackle of the lantern flame a sharp staccato, the occasional splash of a fish an accent, his stone zinging over his blade a percussion. He even begins to hum low in the back of his throat, an old tune he remembers hearing as a child but can't quite place when or where he ever heard it.

> *Come and sway with me*
> *For I lost myself in a cloud*
> *Where the riverbed winds and the trees bend time,*
> *Come sway with me.*
>
> *Come and sway with me*
> *No one ever lost their heart in a storm.*
> *Where the eye look on in a calm so strong,*
> *Come sway with me.*

Enfolded as he is in his own world, he doesn't notice the singing right away. It blends so cleanly into the tune he is humming, folds itself neatly inside of it, that Leon can't say when exactly he realized another voice had joined his own. When he does notice it, he immediately stops humming and stops sharpening his blade to look around, expecting Cassiopeia or Loupe to have joined him, but no. He is as alone now as when he first padded his way up here in bare feet. Only, he isn't alone, if the haunting voice dancing over the waves is any indication.

Leon rises from his seat, turning to face the direction the song seems to echo from, and he follows after it as though compelled. At the ship's prow, the voice is louder and impossibly more beautiful, dancing over the waves like a phantom. Yet Leon feels anything but fearful.

Come and sway with me,
On this cloud I call my own.
Where the daffodils swim and the lochs stand grim,
Come sway with me.

Come and sway with me
Bring me the rain on my doorstep.
Where the hailstorm fails and the snowfall melts,
Come sway with me.

"So, you hear it, too."

"Captain?"

Guadeloupe came onto deck without Leon even realizing it. His booted feet make solid thumps as he makes his way to Leon.

"I haven't heard one since I was a boy," he says as he reaches the rail. His hands brace on the wood as he leans forward.

Leon turns to look at Loupe.

"One of them?"

"The Chinese called them Rényú, ocean spirits. The Greeks called them sirens. Most people know them as merfolk. Mermaids, if you will? But you already know the stories. We all do. Though if the tenor of this voice is any indication, it's probably a male."

Leon stiffens. Red scales, black hair, and tanned skin...

"Get out of here," scoffs Leon, trying to sound skeptical. "You been in the spirits or something? You know mermaids don't come near the surface this far from land."

"I am very much sober, Leon, and yes. How else do you explain a voice like that? And don't tell me it's just the wind. The last I checked, the sea breeze doesn't know human language, let alone sing it. And don't try and sound tough. You wouldn't have been standing here looking out over the water like that if you didn't wonder at least a little bit."

Looking like what?

The song continues, and Leon chews on his lower lip.

"I always thought they were just scary stories told to sailors to keep them from getting the clap from seaside prostitutes."

Loupe scoffs.

"No, they are very much real even if no one believes the legends anymore. Why we have one serenading our ship though, I couldn't even begin to guess."

Leon swallows, his nerves rising into his throat.

"I think one of them saved my life today."

"Impossible."

Leon's eyes narrow. "Lou, I'm telling you, I think one of them—"

"It's not possible, Leon. The merfolk are killers. That's all. Whatever you think happened while you were in the water today was a mixture of shock and adrenaline, not the mercy of a mermaid."

"But..."

Leon's protest dies on his tongue. What does it matter? Loupe is probably right.

"My father was taken by one when I was a boy."

"Really?"

Loupe nods.

"I heard the song and went to listen. I almost went into the water myself, but my pa, he came and stopped me. Shoved me inside the cabin and locked me in. The singing was so powerful, it nearly drove me mad. That's when I heard the splash. He'd jumped into the water to meet her and never came back."

"I'm sorry, Loupe."

"Eh, it was a long time ago."

Loupe points his pistol out to sea and fires. The singing ceases, the source of it frightened away by the gunshot.

"Loupe!"

"Go to sleep, Leonito. You can thank me tomorrow when you're not sleeping with the fishes."

As his captain shuffles his way back to his cabin, Leon returns below deck to his cot. He rustles back and forth for a bit before sleep finally sinks into his bones, and if the lull of a song echoes in his head, he'll make sure to keep it to himself.

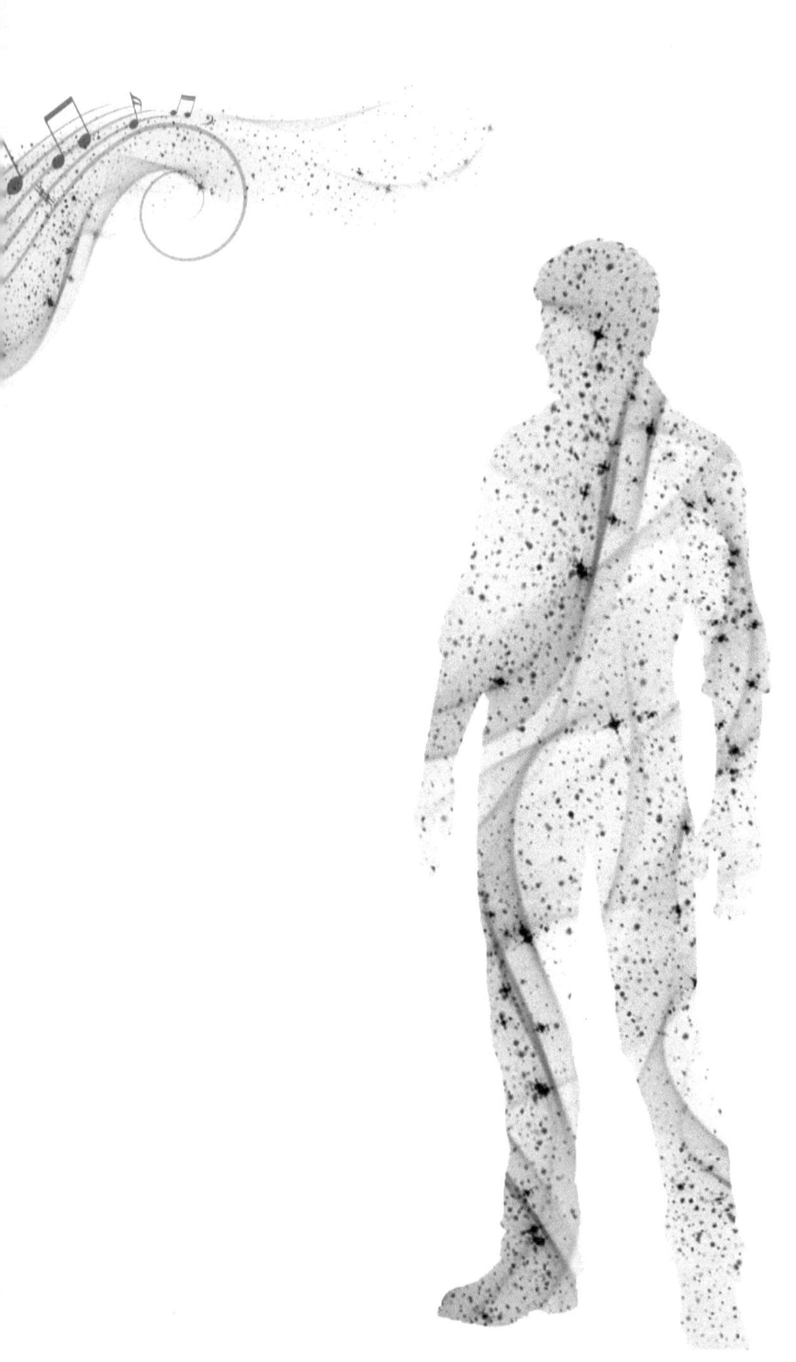

2

Fiddler's Green

THEY DOCK AT CALYPSO CITY THE NEXT evening, and Izacc, Cassiopeia, and Yoshi are quick to drag Leon to shore for some proper celebration. What are they celebrating exactly? Leon doesn't know, but something to do with his "miraculous escape from death" according to Loupe who had opted to stay with the *C-Devil*. He doesn't want to go, preferring to stay at the ship while his mates carry on with their usual romps at port. The noise and stupidity of a bunch of drunkards with too much coin and nothing better to do with it other than spend it on food, women, and wine are not appealing to Leon, but here he is, sitting in a seedy bar, surrounded by seedy patrons, and seedy tavern wenches looking to make a quick coin.

But at least the rum is palatable, and watching Izacc get slapped by nearly every woman he approaches is good enough entertainment for the time being. Later, while his mates are enjoying themselves, he'll take the time to find them some work. Maybe he'll catch wind of a few good rumors of merchant vessels or a new outpost being established by the League after a hexen raid.

Cassiopeia pulls a laughing girl into her lap, nearly upending Leon's drink. He glares at the lady pirate who just shrugs in apology.

It's not like this is the first time Leon has been dragged wenching. It happens occasionally, though he isn't one to glance twice at the women. Leon had been seventeen when the pirate crew who abducted him deemed him man enough to have a proper lady deflower him. His then captain had even had the girls parade themselves in front of him. When the man had noticed Leon's utter lack of interest for the girls, he gave a nod to the matron, who gave Leon a gentle smile before sashaying away only to return with a dark-skinned Hispanic girl, only a few years older than Leon wearing a strange half-pant, half-corset style dress. She seemed pretty enough until Leon had gotten an actual good look at her to notice that "she" was actually a "he" dressed in women's clothing and wearing makeup, and that was that.

The older boy had been kind enough, patient and instructive, and Leon, at least, knew he hadn't hurt the prostitute if the sounds he made had been any indication, but sex with strangers is still mostly unappealing to Leon. Sex with paid whores even more so.

"It's mutually beneficial, Lee. You get a good scratch, and they get your gold. Everyone wins."

Paying for a lay doesn't feel like much of a win to Leon. Not that he thinks of his activities between the sheets as a competition where there are winners and losers to begin with. That's why, while Izacc is gifted with his third slap across the face in as many minutes and Cassi's girl, seeing this, delivers one of her own before traipsing away, Leon contents himself to drink the swill that passes for rum in the fine establishment and counts cards while Yoshi gambles away his earnings just like any other night at port.

At least that's how it is supposed to be until *he* walks in.

Leon doesn't notice him right away since he enters with a group of about eight other men, but the sound of shy laughter carries across the bar like a love song, just resonant enough to draw his attention.

The man's back is turned to him, but he's tall, long limbed and willowy, with long black hair that reaches all the way down to a trim, belted waist, skin the color of warm toffee. He seems to be of Asian lineage as well, wearing a traditional cotton robe in a simple gray and red patterning. Leon can see a coral pendant hanging from his belt and a necklace decorated with seashells around his neck. He wears a single thin braid in his hair, woven through with red string and beaded with colorful and expensive looking seashells. What kind of man would dare to wear something so fine here?

Predictably, the man is quickly accosted by several gentlemen, though he seems to handle himself easily enough, talking them off. They are left in his wake, looking more than a little stunned, and Leon is curious how he has managed that. His question is answered when he finally gets a look at the man's face. And what the fuck! How could someone so obviously pretty show up in such a place as this?

Perfectly almond shaped eyes in a dark chocolate tone are framed by high cheekbones, a delicate jawline, and lips so red Leon wonders if he is wearing lipstick. A small mole dots the corner of his lip.

Their eyes meet, and Leon forgets how to breathe as the man's eyes narrow to half-moons in the wake of the most enchanting smile he has ever seen. He never thought a man could be described as beautiful. Handsome, stunning, gorgeous, cute, yes, but beautiful? This man is beyond any that Leon has ever set his eyes on.

"Leon? Oh, Leon? Hello, anyone home?"

Yoshi flicks him on the forehead, and Leon jerks backward.

"What the hell, Yosh!"

"Whew, thought we lost you there for a minute. Where'd you go?"

Leon looks back in the beautiful man's direction and is disappointed to find that he has turned away again and is now leaning down to speak to one of the sailors he came in with. Izacc follows Leon's gaze and nearly chokes on his ale.

"Holy damn! Look at the peach on that missy. Now that is a sight for sore eyes."

Yoshi turns to look as well and nearly snorts up his liquor.

"I don't think that's a 'missy,' Izacc."

"No, that is definitely a woman. No man is that pretty—"

Izacc chokes again as the man straightens and turns around, making very obvious the flat plane of his chest and the full extent of his height. Leon tracks him as he moves across the room. He seems very careful about where he sets his feet as he walks to claim a seat closer to the band currently playing a raucous drinking song.

"You're right, nevermind. Forget I said anything." Izacc devolves to muttering under his breath as he contemplates his liquor. At this point, Cassiopeia joins in with a laugh, patting Izacc on the shoulder.

"You're right, Izacc. He is very pretty, but I don't think our Leon would have paid him a second glance if he was a woman. As it is, he can't seem to look away from him."

"Shut up, Cass!" Leon growls under his breath before sinking down into his chair and taking a long drag from his tankard. The conversation steers away from the handsome stranger and toward more common topics like supply runs and finding contracts. Izacc, apparently tired of being slapped around, even goes to investigate a table where some bigshot seems to be looking for a vessel to contract. Cassiopeia, on the other hand, disappears with her girl from earlier.

Leon steals glances at the stranger far more often than he would ever admit. He doesn't drink or eat anything, but he does engage in conversation with the people who approach him. He claps along to the band's music no matter the fact that the later the night progresses, the worse their tuning becomes. He doesn't realize how apparent he is being until Yoshi sidles up next to him, uncharacteristically cheery considering he just lost another game of flip jack and five doubloons with that.

"Why don't you go over and talk to him?"

"I don't want to."

"Oh, please! You've been staring at him since he walked into the bar. Just go talk to him. Maybe ask him to dance. It's not like he's accepted anyone else's advances."

Leon lets out a sound that is halfway between a sigh and a hiss.

"Go away, Yoshi."

"Leon," whines the other man back at Leon. "Stop being a guppy and go talk to him."

"Just because you like fucking around doesn't mean everyone else does."

"Maybe, but I bet you'd take pleasure in him if the way you are undressing him with your eyes is any indication."

Yoshi waggles his eyebrows at Leon suggestively, and Leon refrains from punching the witch in the face. He settles for pushing him backward off his chair. Yoshi goes down laughing, nearly busting a rib by the sound of it, as Leon turns back to the stranger who is, suspiciously enough, looking straight at Leon. He isn't sure if he imagines it or not, but the man winks at him, tilting his head in a beckoning manner before returning to watching the band and the drunken dancers on the floor.

Without further ceremony, Leon downs what's left of his rum and rises from his chair. He hears Yoshi whooping behind him, "That's right, Leonito. Get your dick wet!" and ignores him. He shouldn't have pulled his punch earlier. He'll get him later.

In the meantime, he finds himself pulling a chair out across from the handsome, beautiful stranger who doesn't seem the slightest bit put off by his approach. He even smiles at Leon as though greeting an old friend. He ducks his head down in a small bow as Leon settles himself in his seat. The man doesn't have a drink in hand nor anywhere near him on the table.

"I've never seen you here before. First time in Calypso City?" Leon asks.

"First time walking the port, yeah."

Leon's brow furrows. *What an odd response.* The stranger's eyes turn to him as he answers. Leon suddenly feels very warm.

"Is it a good walk so far?"

The man's eyes crinkle at the edges when he smiles.

"It's noisier than I imagined, and I wasn't prepared for the smell, but the company has certainly improved."

So, it would seem Leon's attention is not unwelcome if the coquettish lilt to his voice is anything to go by. A loud noise draws the beauty's attention away, and Leon looks over to see that one of the tavern wenches is presently offering her oral services to one of the men in a darkened corner.

Leon clears his throat with a cough, drawing back his stranger's attention.

"Hm, are you drinking anything?"

"Just water."

"You had the gall to order water from this barkeep?"

Leon has been to Calypso City enough to know what happens to people who insult this particular establishment's "high quality" alcohol—the poor unfortunate sods tossed into the nearest pig pen.

"Nothing else smells good, and I'd rather not poison myself."

"Fair enough, old man."

Delicate brows rise nearly into his hair. "Old man? What makes you so sure I'm older than you?"

Leon smirks, pleased he's caught on to Leon's teasing.

"Most people I meet are. You also have the air of an older gentleman rather than a kid."

"Oh really? And what air is that?"

"Well, for one, you're drinking water in a pirate bar."

The mystery man laughs, and the sound reminds Leon of the seashell wind chimes his mother would hang on their front porch.

Just then the band strikes up a jig, one that Leon knows the step pattern to.

"Would you like to dance?"

The man's cheeks flush a shade of pink that is all too charming despite the dull yellow light of the bar.

"I don't know how."

Leon stands up and holds out his hand.

"I'll show you."

The man worries at his bottom lip nervously. The impulse that surges into his teeth to bite into that soft flesh is terribly compelling, but then his handsome stranger's hand slides into his own, and he is too busy noticing how much smaller that hand is to carry on that thought. His fingers close around the entire width of it; he can feel every knuckle and bone beneath soft uncalloused skin so very unlike his own. As Leon pulls the stranger onto his feet, he seems unsteady despite not being even remotely in the drink, so Leon keeps a solid hold on him, even going so far as to take his other hand in his.

Leon shuffles backward and sideways toward the center of the room where most of the dancing men and women have collected. He sets the pair of them on the outer edge to coach his dance partner through the basic footwork of the dance, several hopping kicks followed by woven footwork that the man copies back to him. He does well, diligently watching and learning, and eventually he relaxes enough to enjoy just moving his body on the dance floor. They don't hold hands or link arms or anything, but they don't stray far from one another either, circling each other amid the other dancers moving around.

But then the music picks up, and the drunks floating throughout the bar get even more excitable. One of the girls collides with Leon's dance partner, and it sends the man tumbling off balance. Leon is there though. He wraps his arms around the man's waist and pulls him bodily into him, lining them up with Leon's front to the thinner man's back. He trips over his own feet again, but Leon keeps him upright.

"S-sorry," he gasps.

Leon laughs. It's endearing how much he seems to fret over his balance, like a lad just gaining his sea legs.

"Follow me. I won't let you fall."

"I am in your hands, *monsieur corsaire*."

Leon's brow arches, real interest now stirring in the pit of his stomach as the stranger, despite being taller and older, submits to his care so readily. Leon sets a firmer hold around a waist so small he can wrap both his hands entirely around it. Leon moves them through the crowd of sweaty bodies and alcohol soaked limbs. He guides and commands at once, grinds into his dance partner's backside, and manipulates him into the correct forms while keeping an eye on the other men and women around them.

Eventually, he turns his partner so they are facing each other and finds half-lidded eyes, blown pupils, and flushed cheeks.

"What's your name?" he asks Leon, and they are so close Leon can feel the fan of the other male's breath over his face.

"I'm afraid I can't tell you that, love."

"Oh, why's that?"

"Just the way it has to be, but you can always tell me yours."

He laughs as Leon spins him in a wide circle.

"Why should I tell you my name when you won't tell me yours?"

"Because I'm handsome and charming."

"More like arrogant and insufferable."

"You love it though."

"Do I?"

"I bet you do, and when I win that bet, you'll tell me your name when you're ready to admit it."

"Mmm."

The fact that Leon has to look up to meet that hazy gaze is more of a turn on than he expected it would be, and he's too punch drunk to resist the temptation in front of him. He rises onto the balls of his feet and kisses his mysterious stranger, right there in the middle of the bar.

There are catcalls and wolf whistles, but it hardly matters.

Those lips are as plump and full as he imagined. There is also, he notes, a distinct lack of the synthetic taste of lipstick he expected. The man tastes like the ocean, clean and laced with freedom, and Leon feels like he is riding the highest crest all the way back to shore. Leon parts his lips, and his tongue flicks out across those impossibly red lips, but before he can deepen their connection, some burly thug has the audacity to shove Leon's partner sideways.

"Get lost, ya poof!"

Leon barely catches him around the waist, though when a hard shove meets his own shoulder, they both end up on the floor.

"Why don't you and your little whore piss off somewhere else? No one here wants to see that shit, faggots!"

The band has stopped playing, and for the most part, people have cleared away. Leon picks himself up off the ground, glaring at the oversized white man wearing a white tunic and blue trousers who has just shoved them. He is wearing a headscarf in the most sickening shade of puke yellow Leon has ever seen.

Leon glances around as he stands. The guy seems to have at least four other crewmates lingering on the periphery. He can't see Izacc anywhere, but Cassiopeia and Yoshi are seated at the bar. Both of his crewmates are looking over, and Cassiopeia has a hand braced over her cutlass, one foot already on the floor. Leon flicks his fingers to let them know everything is fine for now. Behind him, he hears his dance partner shuffling his way to his feet.

"I'm sorry. I must've misheard you. What did you just call us?"

"What? You deaf too, wanker? I called you and your whore a pair of faggots, one cyborg bitch and one chink fairy is what I'm saying."

Leon's fist clenches to punch the brute in the face, but a hand settles on Leon's shoulder, and a musical voice whispers into his ear,

"Hey, it doesn't matter. Let's just leave."

Leon's rage cools but doesn't diminish at the gentle coaxing. Leon lifts a hand to the man's cheek as he turns to look him in the eye. A moment passes between them that Leon can't explain. It unfurls like a sun coral looking for the light of dawn.

"Well ain't you just about *perty* enough to pass for a woman."

The moment bursts, and the puke scarf asshole has returned. Leon turns a gaze hard enough to cut steel on the scumbag. Behind him, his stranger's body tenses, and Leon can feel the nerves rolling off him in waves. Despite that though, the man forces a smile as he addresses the brute.

"Sorry to disturb, but we don't want any trouble. We'll be going now."

At the sound of his silky voice, the thug blinks stupidly, much like the other men Leon had seen approach the beauty earlier. Only this one doesn't seem to take the dismissal for what it is. The puke-scarf-wearing thug clicks his tongue and eyes the lean male from head to toe. Leon's blood boils.

"You know, they say dem Chinaman ain't got much to show as far as equipment goes. Say how 'bout you leave this wanker to himself and spend your evening with me and me mates? I bet we can pay better, too."

"I'm not selling anything."

"Even better."

Greasy fingers reach forward, and the other pirate's teeth crack as Leon's fist meets his jaw.

"You right bastard!"

Leon ducks down to avoid the swing of the asshole's arm and surges upward, ramming his elbow into the thug's chin.

A third strike comes from behind as the mystery man delivers a booted kick directly to the thug's balls.

"Fuckers!"

Somebody whoops across the room, "Fight!" and a shot rings out into the ceiling.

Leon grabs his, apparently, feisty date's forearm, ducks down, and starts to weave them out of the brawl. Women are screaming, men cursing, and the barkeep has already pulled out his own gun. One of the thug's crewmates tries to cut Leon off, but he just reels back and kicks him in the face before shuffling in the direction of the stairs.

"This way," shouts Leon, pulling on the arm still in his grip.

"Where are we going?" the other man shouts over the noise.

"Just keep moving. I've got you."

Yoshi jumps onto his feet with a howl as he too joins in the fun. Cassiopeia, he can't find. Either she is in the thick of the mess, or she's set herself behind a pillar. While he is looking, he doesn't notice a pirate armed with a chair heading directly for him, but he does hear him yell. Leon's head turns, and he lifts an arm to block the blow only to see a small hand thrust forward from behind him. The heel of it breaks the pirate's nose, and the thug drops like a lead weight, the chair falling on top of his head.

Wide chocolate eyes meet Leon's when he looks back.

"Nice hit, *dulce*."

The blush returns and, with it, Leon's smirk.

"Somebody get those motherfuckers!"

Puke Scarf points a pistol straight at them.

"Get down!"

Leon ducks them behind an overturned table as the shots ring out. The motherfuckers are opening fire on them which means this isn't just a bar brawl anymore. They're out for blood. Leon draws his pistol. Activating his vision optics, he aims into the space behind him and fires off two shots before peeking around the corner. Two shots fired, two thugs down, and the oversized thug spots him. Just as the big lug moves to go after them, a bottle breaks against the side of his face, and Leon finds Yoshi's laughing face on the other side of it.

"Lee, get the hell outta here! Cassi, hurry up with that table dresser."

A body goes flying across the room straight through a table. Cassiopeia gives him a salute which Leon returns before looking back at his date as a few of the thugs begin to throw hands their direction.

"Come on."

Leon guides his companion up the stairs, taking them two at a time as the thugs start to give chase despite Leon's crewmates. Leon breaks open the door to the roof as a shot fires in their direction. Once they are both through, Leon slams the door shut and braces it with a plank while the taller man presses his weight against it.

"You have some pretty amazing friends."

"My crew," Leon replies with a smile. "Yeah, they are pretty great."

BAM! BAM!

"Open up, you bloody bilge rats before I cut out your spleens!"

Sounds like Puke Scarf.

Leon pulls the lithe male away from the door, backing up while scanning the streets for an out. They aren't so high up that a jump off the roof would kill them, but it would definitely hurt, and considering his handsome companion's penchant for falling at the slightest disturbance, it probably wouldn't be a good idea.

The city's nightlife is in full bloom: cars whiz through the streets, motorcycles rev back and forth, and robots buzz by on their various errands. He spots a courier drone pushing along a delivery crate in midair. It gives him an idea.

"Do you trust me?"

Brown eyes look at him, slightly panicked but also bright with excitement and far too open for their own good. Shit!

He doesn't even know Leon's name, yet the pirate is asking him if he trusts him. How much more messed up can he get?

"Yes." The man's voice pulls him from his musings, and Leon looks up in surprise. "Yes, I trust you."

He shouldn't though. He really, really shouldn't.

Leon shifts his gun into his right hand and grips the other man by the forearm. He pulls them both to the edge of the roof just as the men from the bar are climbing their way up. The other man nearly trips, but Leon keeps him steady. He fires two shots, turns to the other man, and says, "Don't look down."

Then he jumps, cradling the other in his arms. They land in a heap in the drone's cart full of what looks to be somebody's groceries. Leon grunts as he lands flat on his back with the weight of the other on his chest, but at least the bags of bread and (oops) eggs cushion his landing enough that he doesn't think he'll have any bruises to show for it.

The drone stutters at the added weight, but a few adjustments to its systems and it sputters on like the little engine that could.

More gun shots ring out, and Leon hears the whooping and hollering as several men get tossed out onto the street on their backsides. Leon holds a finger to his lips as the beauty across his chest looks askance at him. He gets the message because lays his head back on Leon's chest.

Leon sighs in relief as the cargo crate keeps moving forward, and before long, the bar thugs are a distant memory as the drone takes them farther toward the port.

This is about the moment when Leon realizes he has made a tactical error. He is now lying beneath the very warm, very svelte body of a man he is highly attracted to, and in the aftermath of a bar fight, his adrenaline high is beginning to shift into arousal. Already his pants tighten, growing more uncomfortable by the second. He wonders if his heartbeat is audible to his present company considering that head of silky-smooth black hair is still resting on his chest.

The drone takes a sharp turn toward the pier, and the pair are jostled closer into each other. A dull hardness prods his thigh. It would seem he is not the only one affected by the close proximity. The beauty lifts his head from Leon's chest, and Leon's gaze darkens as pretty brown eyes meet his. The gleam he finds there must be a reflection of the moon. It's otherworldly and enticing, and when those seemingly bottomless irises flash at him, he sees naught but a mirror of his own heightening lust.

Leon's hands fist into the collar of the robe and tug. He nearly groans as their mouths clash in the most volatile kiss Leon has ever been a party to.

"Gods, you are a dream," says Leon, drunk on this feeling, ready to dive back into those lips.

Suddenly, the crate comes to a stop, and the little drone buzzes off to alert the person it was delivering groceries to.

"But if this were a dream, we wouldn't be able to see it through to the end." The beauty grabs the adept by his hair and claims the pirate's lips. This kiss is too short, too heated, and too much to not be a precursor to something more. "And I very much want to see this dream through to the end."

Leon hurls himself upward and out of the cart. Laughter follows him, but he reaches up to help his partner from the crate through his elation, and then Leon is laughing too as he tugs him down the docks. He knows what he's looking for, knows there is bound to be one here, and he spots it at the tail end of the dock, a covered rowboat just big enough for two people, tied off and well enough away from prying eyes to give them the privacy they desire. He jumps down into the small boat, rips the tarp aside, and is pleased to find a pile of relatively soft netting and toss-away fabrics tangled up at the bottom. He reaches up to his companion.

"Come on down, *mon haut.*"

Leon catches him in his arms and is on him not a moment later, stripping away cloth and leather and any other offensive barriers between him and his prize before guiding the man down gently into the nest of soft goods. Tanned skin shimmers in the moonlight, and the body below him must be carved from the heavens, too perfect, too delicate, and too much for any mere mortal to withstand. The taller man laughs once more, at once low and effortlessly seductive while being filled with affection and adoration, and Leon understands why he never stopped believing in love at first sight even if it only lasts for one night.

Then, there is nothing between them but the push and pull of sex, the drag of skin against skin, the give and take of pleasure and heat and passion. The boat rocks under the slide of their bodies as Leon dives into the man's body, determined never again to surface until he's taken his fill of the offering being presented to him.

Riding the tides of euphoria, the sighs and gasps below him resonating like a song in the starlit darkness, Leon realizes he's never taken such pleasure in drowning.

At dawn, Leon collects his belongings and dresses while keeping an eye on the beauty still slumbering, naked save for the robe Leon pulled over the both of them before they slept. He feels heavy now, plagued with the burden of reality daylight brings. All the magic of the night before evaporates in the harsh gleam of the sun.

It doesn't matter.

It doesn't matter that he might like to see him again. It doesn't matter that he might want to get to know him like a proper lover. It doesn't matter that Leon knows without question that he has been struck by Cupid's arrow, well aimed and embedded so deeply into his heart he doesn't think he'll ever manage to pull it out.

It doesn't matter because Leon is a thief at the best of times and a killer at the worst of times and something in between most of the time. And this man...

He's kind and patient and gentle and a force of nature. Funny and clumsy and untamed, and completely unlike anyone Leon has ever met before, and *fuck!* Leon shouldn't even have touched him for risk of tainting something that pure.

Leon's fingers card through soft obsidian tresses once more, unraveling the braid dexterously. He takes the red thread from the man's hair and weaves a thin bracelet out of it. A token to remember him by that Leon winds around the man's thin wrist. It doesn't mean anything. Not to Leon. At least, it won't in a week when Leon is sailing into another port hundreds of leagues from here with only the memory of toffee-colored skin and dark eyes unraveling beneath his touch as company.

He leaves without ever getting his bedmate's name. Names are too personal, too tempting to write into your life and keep there, so he leaves without because he knows better than to ever drag someone into this kind of lifestyle. Cupid and his sick sense of fated love be damned.

3

Pearling for Oysters

YESTERDAY WHEN HE WENT TO SEE HIS mechanic about his arm, she went ahead and added a multitool into his wrist. He decides to test it out now while waiting for his crewmates to get back on deck. Leon sits on the pier whittling his latest carving when Izacc and Yoshi walk up. He glances up from the small hammerhead replica after a long drag of his blade along its body and sees Yoshi fiddling with a holodisk. There are numbers flashing across the projection. Lots of numbers with credit symbols at the end. Numbers far too high in value for a witch as terrible at gambling as Yoshi.

"New credit disk?" Leon calls, eyeing him appraisingly.

Yoshi smiles so wide his eyes close.

"Oh, I just suggested to the dealer that someone was cheating. He rewarded me quite handsomely."

Fucking psionics. Yoshi, for all his witchiness, doesn't seem all that impressive on the surface. He has no physical powers and very little knowledge of spells and incantations; he isn't particularly talented at potions or cooking despite his forays into kitchen witchery. No, Yoshi is a terrible witch by all accounts except for one subtle ability that he milks to the end of the world.

"One day, you're going to get caught playing your mind tricks," calls Loupe from their ship's deck. "And I will not be there to stop them from cutting out your tongue."

"At least I earn my keep," cheeks the witch. He then turns his attention entirely on Leon, sidling up to him and tapping his mechanical arm. "Unlike other people around here. Our mako didn't make it back to the ship last night."

He waggles his eyebrows at him.

"Yoshi," Leon growls.

"Soooo, was it good? It was good, wasn't it? You wouldn't have spent the whole night with him otherwise."

"Fuck off!"

"Haha! Come on, Leon. I didn't stick my neck out in that barfight for nothing. Give us the dirt. Please! I didn't get any action last night."

"How sad for you," Leon deadpans. "May your sacrifice aid you in ascending."

Yoshi opens his mouth aghast.

"Leon De Mares! My cruel younger brother who I give so much to treats me this way!"

Leon is about to treat him to that punch he pulled last night when Loupe shouts.

"Yoshi, leave Leon alone and come help me with your damned foodstuffs! The kitchen is a mess again, and you know that's your responsibility."

"Yes, mom!" Yoshi sighs as he marches up the gangplank. "You're not off the hook, Leonito. I want a full account before we set off."

Leon flips a lewd hand gesture at the retreating male before returning his attention back to his carving. Despite the pestering, a fond smile quirks his lips as he remembers pressing his palms flat along the planes of a firm, heaving chest as he took his bedmate from behind at some point between their second and third round. Maybe he'll tell his nosy crewmate about how the beauty's eyes had sparkled with unshed tears as Leon drove into him for the first time but had been too overwrought to say anything other than soft, panted praises and encouragements into Leon's ear. Yoshi would toss himself overboard if Leon ever actually did spill the dirt on his activities last night.

Izacc, still on the pier, lets out a low whistle. "Wow, you are in a good mood." Leon raises an eyebrow at him. Izacc shrugs. "Normally, you would've punched him in the kidney."

Izacc laughs before jumping up onto a crate behind Leon while the younger returns to his project. He's trying to finish this hammerhead carving before they set out. He just needs the detailing at this point. Izacc babbles on about something or other, but he pays the man no mind, simply nodding or humming at appropriate intervals when expected. The ridges on the snout are going to be the end of him. Why are hammerheads such strangely shaped animals?

"Holy shit!"

Leon's hand slips. The knife slices into the fleshy part of his thumb.

"*Merde*, Iz! Working with a sharp object here!"

He's got all of these mechanical bits and pieces, yet he slices open his organic parts. He sticks his thumb in his mouth and tastes the blood welling. He elbows Izacc in the side, but the man just grips his head and turns him to look at whatever got the man going in the first place.

"Looks like you've got a visitor, Leonito."

Leon nearly careens sideways as the sunlight glints off his most recent bedmate's cascading black hair. Said bedmate who is presently making his way up the dock toward them with a netted sack slung over his shoulder.

"Howling moons, he's even prettier in the daylight!"

Leon is sorely tempted to reach over and punch the lycan, but before he can, his dalliance is upon them and he's yanking his thumb out of his mouth faster than if he were to have just set it on a hot pan. Merciful heavens, he's smiling that same soft smile that made Leon's heart beat a thousand leagues per minute last night.

"Hi," says the beauty pleasantly with a small wave. The threaded bracelet is still there, right where Leon tied it in the small hours before dawn.

"Hi," Leon echoes, feeling more than a little ambushed. Izacc tries to conceal his laughter behind a closed fist. He does a shoddy job of it. "What are you doing here?"

The man shuffles from one foot to the other. "I was hoping to discuss a transaction with you."

Leon's eyes narrow.

"If you're a prostitute, you should learn to barter your pay before, rather than tracking me down all the way to my ship for money that you will not see after."

Izacc physically elbows him in the side with a scathing chide. The nameless beauty doesn't seem to take offense though. He just gives a musical chuckle and answers, "I'm not a prostitute, nor do I want your money. Though it was kind of you to leave the bracelet as a token this morning. I didn't hear you leave."

There is no measure of unkindness or anger in the statement, yet somehow Leon feels like he is being reprimanded for leaving without giving a proper goodbye. Well, bully for him! What did he expect messing around with a pirate? Breakfast in bed and flowers? Not likely! Leon glares at the man who, to his credit, seems entirely unfazed by Leon's chilly countenance. Izacc glances shiftily between the two before clapping Leon on the back.

"Whelp! I'll leave you two to your lover's quarrel. I'm sure the captain needs a hand with something or other. Thanks for taking care of our Leon, stranger. He's in a much better mood today than normal."

"Izacc," hisses Leon as the man ruffles his hair.

"Be nice, Leonito," calls the traitorous bastard as the older man all but sprints up the gangplank, waving over his shoulder as he goes. Great! Now he knows his name. Leon vows right then and there to toss the lycan overboard the next chance he gets. He'll fish him out, of course, but only after he starts begging.

"So, Leon, huh?"

Leon huffs. "Yeah, that's right."

Leon tucks the knife back into its socket on his wrist augmentation, sets the sculpture down, and pats the wood shavings from his pants, careful to avoid aggravating the cut on his left hand but still the sting of it makes him wince. ¡Pinche Cabron! He is going to make sure there are sharks in the water when he throws Izacc into the dip. There is blood covering his entire palm.

"You're bleeding."

"Yeah, Izacc's a right bastard when he wants to be."

In three quick strides, (*damn, does he have long legs!*) the man is in front of him, pulling a thin handkerchief from inside his robes. Slender fingers curl around Leon's hand and lift. The touch sets Leon's skin ablaze, and he nearly yanks his hand out of the man's hold, but he holds on with a gentle firmness that is enough to dissuade Leon from backing away. The man winds the cloth around his thumb methodically as though he were handling something delicate and fragile rather than the calloused hand of a skilled shooter and swordsman.

Brown eyes glance in the direction of the hammerhead carving, sitting with the bloodied knife.

"It's a beautiful carving. You even got the detailing correct on their snouts and the ridging of their backs. Most just see sharks as a set of fins with teeth."

That piques Leon's attention.

"It's hard to forget the details when you've seen one up close."

"On a hook?" asks the beauty as he ties off the knot.

"In the water," answers Leon. "An animal like that deserves respect, not to be fished out of the ocean like a common tuna."

The man hums appreciatively as he finishes tying off the makeshift bandage. It looks ridiculous wrapped around Leon's thumb like a chunky, bloodstained bow.

"You should be more careful, Leon De Mares. Your hands are precious things, you know."

Leon snorts and shakes his head. Precious things look a lot more like the man in front of him, rare gems meant to be tucked away in treasure chests so no one can steal away their shine, and nothing at all like the rough and tumble person that is Leon De Mares. Nothing about him is precious, especially not his hands. Too large, too rough, too scarred from all the shit he's had to claw his way through just to have the option of standing here today. His hands are more machine than they are flesh. *What's so precious about that?*

"They are," the beauty insists. "They make beautiful things."

Those lithe fingertips glance over the back of his hand and wrist, the faintest of touches that inspire goosebumps to form along his arm. He pulls back before the lump in his throat can become even more prominent.

"Thanks but you didn't have to do that."

"I wanted to," he replies, stepping back and away, having read Leon's discomfort.

"Right," says Leon, tucking his hand behind his back. "Well if you're not here for money, what are you here for—and don't tell me you just wanted another taste of my charming personality."

"And if I did?"

Leon smirks. "You'd be disappointed. I'm only charming to people who don't know my name. Everyone else knows I'm a right bastard."

The smile returns, and Leon has a hard time forcing himself not to return it, so he looks away instead, turning his back to the other man.

"Well, then I guess it's a good thing I'm here for a more practical purpose," the beauty says. "I'd like to barter passage on your ship."

Leon's answer is immediate. "Absolutely not."

"Why not?"

"You realize this is a pirate vessel, right? You have no weapons on you, you're pretty enough to be mistaken for a woman, and you clearly have no understanding of men like me otherwise you wouldn't have come here at all. *Desole, mon ami,* but take my advice. You'd be better off waiting for a merchant vessel if you want to leave port. Guppies like you don't belong on a pirate ship."

"Thanks for the advice, but I won't be taking it."

Leon's brow furrows.

"Dealing with merchants is much easier than dealing with pirates for a civilian like you. It'll probably cost you less too."

"I'm not interested in dealing with greedy merchants."

"So, you'd rather deal with greedy pirates?" asks Leon, indignant. *Is this man insane or just delusional?*

"I know I'd rather deal with you."

"You don't know anything about me!" Leon snarls, rounding on the other in a ferocious about-face. To his credit, the beauty doesn't retreat backward, nor does he avert his gaze.

"No," he answers calmly. "And yet still I trust you."

"Then you're a fool," Leon spits, and despite his aggressive posturing, he feels like an absolute ass when the man finally recoils. His thoughts are a mess of surprise, elation, horror, and, of all the stupid things, lust as the man chews on his lower lip, long eyelashes fluttering as he pointedly avoids Leon's gaze. Perhaps he's shouted some good sense into the man. No civilian in their right mind would ever deal with a pirate, not unless they had something they needed to hide. The wind blows his long hair aside, and Leon sees with no uncertainty the small hickey he left under the beauty's left ear just hours ago already turning purple.

He watches the man's chest rise and fall in a deep, fortifying inhale and exhale before he finally speaks, meeting Leon's gaze head on.

"Look, I know you think you have me all figured out, but there is a lot about me that you don't know. "

So, he does have something to hide. Figures. Who doesn't? Question is whether or not what he's hiding is worth too much to leave behind. Leon kicks the heel of his boot into the boarding at his feet with a bitter laugh, turning to face out to sea, keeping the man in his peripheral vision while lacing his fingers behind his head.

"Am I supposed to be hoping for the opportunity to learn those things?"

"That's entirely up to you, Monsieur." His eyes flash, possessing a challenge of their own. "But I would appreciate it if you would refrain from writing me off just because I let you fuck me into near oblivion last night. I can hold my own in a tough situation as you caught a glimpse of while we were leaving the bar."

Leon crosses his arms across his chest and leans back against the crate. He looks down and away in shame for treating this man like a child. Leon grits his teeth and resists the urge to keep fighting. He concedes the point, not that that means he is about to give in.

"Fair enough, but that still doesn't mean I'll let you aboard."

"I'm willing to pay, and I doubt your captain will say no to a good investment."

"Che! I doubt you have enough credits in that sack to tickle Loupe's fancy."

The man laughs, digging into his sack.

"I may not have credits, but I have this."

In the man's palm is a black gemstone, dark as pitch, and Leon's eyes widen as in the sunlight, a rainbow of color glitters over the surface.

When Leon was ten years old, he snuck out of the house for an early morning pearl dive.

Up until then, Leon had only ever gone out into the coral reefs scavenging for oysters with other children. The group of three or four children were carefully monitored by a small contingent of mothers on boats whenever they swam their way into the deeper parts of the shallows on small bodyboards.

Oyster harvesting was not dangerous per se, but there were always risks to diving in the reefs: eels, water snakes, small sharks etc., but the risk was worth it if they were able to fill up their sacks with oysters and mussels and clams, each hard won find a lottery ticket just waiting to be cracked open to reveal a nice prize that could be sold at the market for a small fortune. Pearls, for all that they were the waste product of an invertebrate, sold for a pretty penny, and since Leon's family was poor, such endeavors were a necessity to their livelihoods.

But that morning, Leon was alone.

His father was away on a fishing haul, trying to bring in a bounty despite it being the off-season, and Leon was left with his mother—his very sick, very frail mother, who was going to die if they couldn't get her the medicine they couldn't afford.

Leon went out into the surf to brave the reef alone, determined to scavenge as many oysters as he could from the rocky bottom of the ocean. He was a strong swimmer. He could manage. He needed to do this. He didn't have a choice anyway.

He was doing well. He'd nearly filled his sack, but with dawn breaching the horizon, Leon knew that he would need to paddle back in soon before high tide set in, but with his mother's health on his mind, he went down for another dive thinking he could outrace the incoming tide.

He misjudged.

High tide barreled in with such fury that there was nothing he could do to prevent himself from being carried off by the riptide. He was too small, too young, and too inexperienced to deal with the battering of the waves against his body.

The current pulled him under and thrashed him about. As his vision darkened, all he could think about was his mother alone and still asleep without any idea where her son might have gone. He saw the rock bed hurtling up toward him, and braced for impact. Right before he lost consciousness, he heard something like a song being sung into his ear, and he never felt the impact of the rock as the lack of oxygen made him black out.

"Leon!"

Leon sputtered awake to the sound of his mother's screams. She hovered over him, the dark bruises under her eyes a stark contrast to how pale the rest of her face was. She shouldn't have been out of bed. Why was she out of bed?

"Leon! Thank the goddess. You're okay."

"Mum?"

The sun was high in the sky. He was on the beach. He must have washed up while he was unconscious, but he was leagues away from shore. The tide should have carried him out to sea. He moved to sit up, and his whole body ached something painful.

"What were you doing out there by yourself? You could have drowned! My son could have drowned. Someone get the doctor."

"Mom, no! I'm fine."

"No, you are not, young man. I wake up this morning to an empty house, your father's paddle boat gone, and high tide crashing into the shore hard enough to bludgeon a seagull. You had me scared to death."

His mom ranted and fussed over him while he opened his satchel. Most of the oysters he harvested were gone, washed away in the surf. He wanted to scream. All of that for nothing. He nearly threw the bag away from him when he spied something shimmering at the bottom of the bag. A gemstone by the looks of it, about the diameter of his pinky. Almost like a black pearl, but it shone in a rainbow of colors, luminescent and glittering in the sunlight.

He held it up to the light and wondered at how indescribably pure it looked. He didn't pick that up from the reef bottom. He turned it in his hand.

It looked like a teardrop.

That single pearl fetched Leon's family enough money to cover the cost of his mother's medical expenses. She beat her illness, and for a few more years, Leon's home life was the picture of happiness.

But these things don't last.

Just days after his thirteenth birthday, Leon would take his first steps into manhood by accompanying his father out to sea on the little fishing barge his father was fortunate enough to call his own. His mother had cried with both pride and sorrow as Leon took his first steps onto the small ship, a fishing net slung over his shoulder and a pack under his arm. He would hug his mother goodbye and say "see you soon" not knowing that he would never see his home again. Three days into their fishing trip, pirates attacked his father's vessel, and Leon, the lone survivor of the attack, found himself a cabin boy on a pirate ship. It's how he met Cassiopeia, Loupe, Yoshi, and Izacc.

It's how he became what he is today.

It's how, years down the line, he finds himself standing on *C-Devil*'s gangplank looking down at the open palm of a man holding the exact same gem that once saved his mother's life. The exact same gem that he found after nearly drowning himself in a riptide at the tender age of ten.

"How do you have that?"

"It's mine," is the reply he gets. "Will you take it as payment or not? I hear that you can fetch a good price for it at the right jeweler."

Leon shakes his head.

"You're not wrong. Fine, you can come aboard. But don't touch anything and stay out of the crew's way. If someone asks you to do something, you do it. You get underfoot, you will be stepped on, and it won't be our problem. We won't be altering our course for your sake, so you'll have to just decide when you disembark on your own."

"Fair enough," he says, repeating Leon's earlier words back to him, and Leon turns around to board, not bothering to check if the man follows him or not.

"It's Thale, by the way. Anders Thale. In case you were wondering my name."

Leon turns once more to give the man an appraising look. Izacc is right. He is far more beautiful in the light of day than he is in a seedy pirate bar, and it doesn't help Leon's irritation how open his countenance is. How can anyone spend any amount of time in a pirate port and still look that pure and innocent?

"I wasn't," he quips.

"Hm. I see. Here I thought pirates liked to know when they've won a bet by having their wagers honored."

Leon freezes.

"You love it, though."

"Do I?"

"I bet you do, and when I win that bet, you'll tell me your name..."

"Not all bets are made with the intention of winning."

"Well, the victory is yours anyway."

"Is that supposed to be a confession?"

"Would you like it to be?"

Leon turns away from Thale then. Whether he is unable or unwilling to answer, he isn't so sure, but deflect he does anyway.

"Go on. I need to introduce you to the captain."

Thale's steps are methodical as he steps up the gang-plank. Watching the other man as he follows him up, Leon realizes that Thale's footsteps are as unsure as his own.

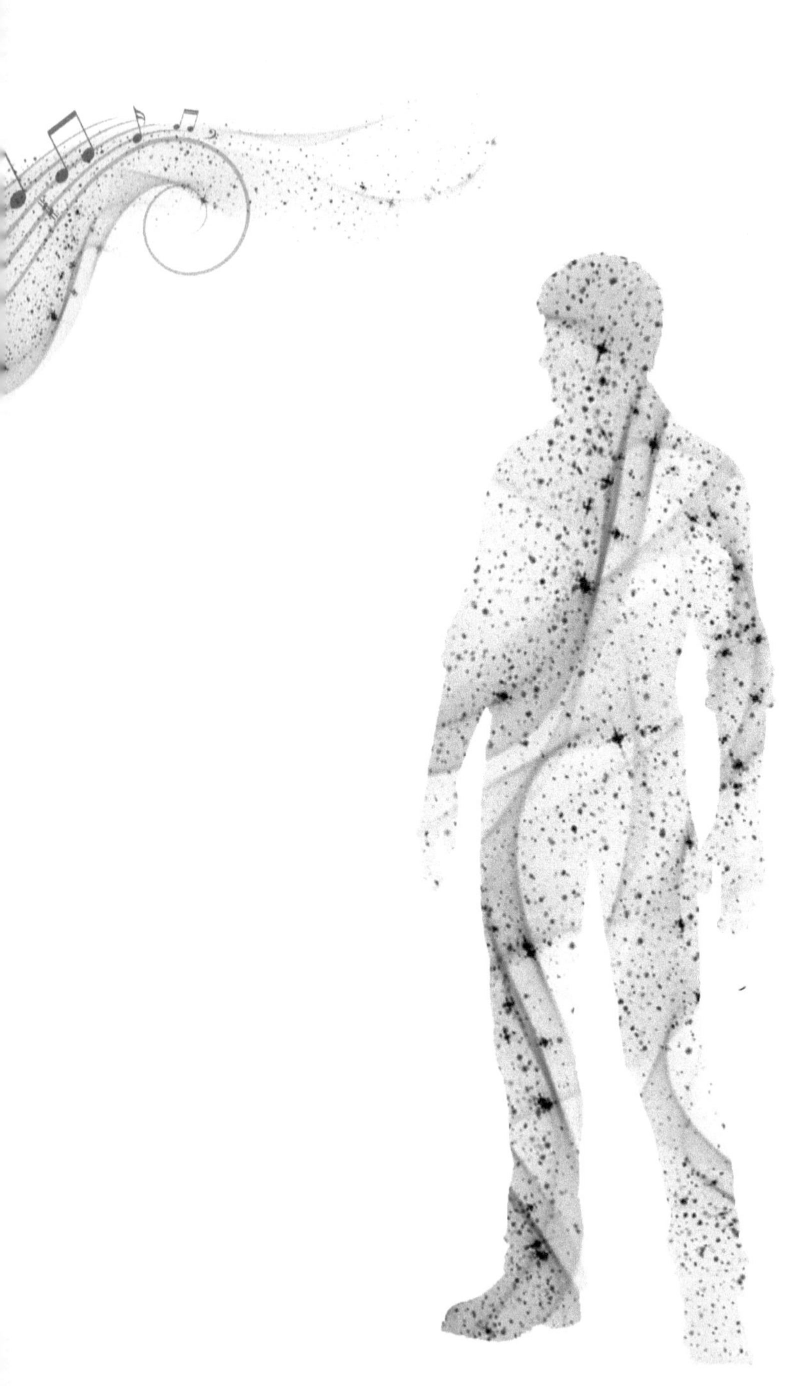

4

Stowaway

LEON AVOIDS THALE LIKE THE PLAGUE after that. Yoshi settles the man below deck, not that he has much to settle, and Cassiopeia returns with another contract passenger, a short, sour-faced white man named Habernathy who has apparently offered Loupe an exorbitant figure as far as payment goes, half of which was paid upfront. He also comes with an entourage of five other men, one of whom is apparently a doctor which was another reason Loupe accepted the contract. The other four Leon doesn't quite like the look of, but Habernathy is prepared to pay some good money to guarantee their spots onboard, and the extra hands are always nice to have. Trophy fishermen from the look of it. They haul aboard netting and ropes and fishing spears and a huge glass tank that Habernathy frets over to no end until it is carefully anchored down in one corner of the main deck where it won't be in the way of any actual work.

Finally, after all of that, they set sail, Loupe at the helm. They leave Calypso City behind, lighter in their pockets but heavier on their supplies. Not to mention heavier for the number of bodies on board. Habernathy has done his part loading them with enough foodstuffs and supplies to compensate for his additional people. Thale seems content to mind his own business, though he is quick to oblige when Loupe asks him to take care of any simple task their captain deems fit to assign him.

Leon isn't paying much attention to his own, working through untangling some rope and too busy looking over at where Thale is swabbing the deck to notice the warning hiss when a little white paw lashes out and four sharp claws dig into the metal on the back of his hand.

"Ouch, what the—!"

He ducks down to look inside the tangle of rope to see a scrunched up, furry, round face with large amber eyes glaring at him. The cat hisses at him as though Leon had done anything to deserve the feline's ire. Yoshi, noticing Leon's yelp, ambles over and peers into the apparent cat bed that has been made out of their lines.

"Looks like we have a stowaway, mates," he calls out. "Hey isn't it supposed to be good luck if a cat wanders onto your ship? Here, kitty kitty—Ow!"

Yoshi's hand meets the same fate as Leon's as the little devil cat scratches him too.

"Hellcat then. Got it. Somebody get a net or something to fish the thing out."

Yoshi is mostly just joking, but after three other people try to get the cat out of the rope coils and fail—one person even gets a nice bite on the wrist for their efforts—Leon wonders if they are going to have to wrangle the little beast out after all.

"Alright, somebody give me a pistol. I'm going to shoot the dang thing."

One of Habernathy's men, Carrow says this after getting bitten, already reaching for a gun when Thale runs over.

"Wait. Hold on. You don't need to kill it."

"Look, the cat is not budging, and we need those ropes. You want to reach in there and wrestle it out, be my guest. If not, then let the professionals deal with it."

Leon rolls his eyes. *Yes, the guy is a real professional.*

"She's just frightened. Give me a minute. I'll get her out."

Izacc crooks his arms over Leon and Yoshi's shoulders.

"I bet you ten credits he gets scratched."

Yoshi shrugs as Thale kneels in front of the rope nest while gesturing for everyone to back up a bit. It's a little odd the way he goes to sit, angling himself sideways on his right hip with his legs half-extended to his left.

"You're on. I bet he gets bitten."

Leon isn't quite sure why his crewmates betting on Thale's failure bothers him, but he expresses as much by upping the ante.

"Double it, and he succeeds."

"Oh ho ho! Our mako, betting in his fine doxy's favor. How chivalrous of you, Leo, supporting your boyfriend!"

Izacc gets a hard elbow to the ribs for his troubles. He wheezes exuberantly but happily accepts that he'll be forty credits richer in just a few minutes if the growling coming from inside the ropes is any indication that Thale is very much about to reap his words. He even preens about it until Thale holds a hand out to the animal and begins to hum. Everyone shuts up as his voice wraps around the entire crew.

The humming seems to calm the furious animal because the hissing and spitting ceases.

"That's right. It's safe," Thale coos at the animal as though speaking to a precious babe, and Leon watches astonished as a little white and gray munchkin cat peeks out from the rope coils to give a sniff at Thale's fingertips. And then, like magic, the cat steps out of its nest and into Thale's waiting arms. How, exactly, such a small creature caused so much trouble, Leon has no idea, but he feels really stupid anyway as the previously ferocious beast purrs in Thale's arms.

"Well, I'll be damned."

Izacc looks gobsmacked. Leon slaps him on the chest.

"I'll take my winnings off your hands anytime."

"Screw you, Leon."

"In your dreams."

"Ah, excuse me," Thale calls over to them. He shifts from one foot to the other seemingly uncomfortable or off balance. "But, um, is there fish anywhere? I think she's hungry."

"That cat won't be much of a ratter if you overfeed it."

Loupe comes up behind Thale and claps him on the shoulder. Thale laughs. It bubbles up out of his throat, an uncomfortable sound, and he leans away from the captain, touch shy.

"I'll keep that in mind."

Reading the man's body language, he drops his palms to his side and bows his head in apology.

"That was mighty impressive though, I have to admit. Leon, why don't you show Thale to the galley? I'm sure he'll find what he needs there."

Leon's head shoots up in mild panic.

"But Yoshi is in charge of foodstuffs."

"I'm asking you."

Leon doesn't bother hiding his glare.

Just hours ago, Loupe had taken one glance at the gem Thale had bartered for passage aboard the *C-Devil* and agreed to the deal. It certainly doesn't help that Thale is so naturally charismatic, Loupe took an immediate liking to him.

Leon feels betrayed, especially as the others snicker under their breath at him. They must have told Loupe exactly who Thale is, and judging by the mischievous sparkling in Loupe's eye, he is very much doing this on purpose.

Leon does not find it amusing.

"Monsieur...?"

"De Mares is fine. That's my last name," he gruffs.

"Very well, Monsieur De Mares." Leon makes a noise of annoyance before ambling forward. He tosses his head at

Thale as an indication to follow before heading below deck. He doesn't bother double-checking that the man follows.

The *C-Devil's* galley is small but functional, and considering they just left port, Yoshi has everything freshly stocked. Dried herbs hang from the ceiling bar, stiff salted rye breads sit piled in a basket, bags of rice and wheat flour lean against the back wall. There are also dried meats and fruits hung on the central pillar, and the fridge is stuffed to near overflowing with perishables. The oven that Yoshi uses to cook is unlit and clean, prepped for their voyage's needs. Glass bottles of various cooking oils line the walls, anchored down with fishing line.

"Let's see. Yoshi always keeps a stock of canned fish somewhere around here. Not much more fit for a cat that I can think of. Ah! Here we go."

Leon fishes a tin can out of one of the cabinets, then uses a multitool on his left index finger to cut the lid open.

"Hope he doesn't mind tuna."

Thale's jingling chuckle gives him pause.

"What's so funny?"

"It's a girl."

"Oh... Well, I hope her majesty is happy with her dinner."

He passes the can to Thale. Almost immediately, Thale scrunches up his nose and actually gags, turning his head away from the open can.

"That smells awful."

Leon raises an eyebrow at that. It smells fine to him.

"It smells like canned tuna fish."

"It smells rotten is what it smells like."

Rotten?

Leon dips a finger in the can and gives the fish a taste. It tastes just the way it always does. Salty, fishy, tuna-y. Thale's lip curls. Her majesty the cat seems to find it acceptable though because she pokes her head out from where she's buried herself in Thale's robe. Thale sets the can on the countertop with a grimace, and the feline hops out of his arms to happily lap up the offering straight from the can.

Thale looks a little green around the gills watching her. Leon can't hold back the bark of laughter.

"Don't tell me you're a picky eater. Once the fresh food runs out, we'll be living off of this stuff for a good while. I'd hate to see you waste away to nothing."

"I'll fish for myself if I have to, but I doubt any good will come of me eating that."

Leon shrugs. "Suit yourself."

A strong wave must strike the ship's keel because the floor lurches beneath their feet. Leon shuffles his feet and maintains his balance easily enough, but Thale is another story. He flails, trying to keep his feet under him and tumbles sideways right into Leon. It spirals them both into the galley wall while the cat just chases her little tin can of tuna across the counter, still munching as she goes.

Leon winces as his back meets the wall and stars burst in his vision as the back of his head meets a shelf. Thale's hands slap on either side of his head as their chests, hips, and knees collide with shared groans of pain. As the ship rights itself, Thale begins to stumble backward, and Leon instinctively wraps an arm around his waist to keep him from ending up on his ass. Leon's head pounds something fierce, his muscles protesting the usage for anything other than maintaining verticality.

"You are really not good at maintaining your balance, are you?" It comes out as more of a growl than he means, gritting it through the pain in his head instead of just staying quiet.

"S-sorry. I didn't mean to..."

Thale's face flushes an immediate red as he tries to scramble away, but Leon holds fast, screwing his eyes shut as the jostling aggravates his head more.

"Stop moving," he grits out, head still spinning.

Thale stills, and Leon lifts a hand to check his head. Sure enough there is a nice knot forming at his crown.

Leon flinches back as Thale lifts a hand to his face.

"What are you—?"

"Shh..." hushes the other man, eyelashes fanning over his cheekbones as he blinks down at Leon. "Just close your eyes."

Despite his better judgment, Leon does as he's told, more than a little helpless to do otherwise considering the throbbing in his head. Even the dim light of the galley lanterns burn the retinas of his eyes. He probably does have a concussion.

Gentle fingers stroke over the damaged area, threading through his hair and stroking there in soothing, clockwise circles. A warm, tingling sensation crawls up the back of his neck and into the tender area. It's strangely pleasurable like candle wax dripping on his skin or holding his breath for just a few seconds too long underwater. He sucks his lower lip between his teeth and bites down as the sensation intensifies, the rhythm of Thale's tender prods increasing.

Leon loses track of all sense of time as the heat rises and falls through his whole body like waves washing across the shore of his senses until Thale's touch recedes. Unable to help himself, Leon reaches up and cords his fingers through Thale's still tangled in his hair. Leon's eyes slide open to greet concerned dark eyes. If he didn't have a wall to his back and a solid floor under his feet, he'd fall right into them.

"Sorry again," whispers Thale. "You should feel better now."

Leon hums his thanks, too blissed-out to form coherent language. Warm body, pretty, pretty face, his own limbs light and airy as if he were swimming. He could just eat those pouty red lips, drag his teeth down that long neck, perhaps suck a darker bruise into the flesh that still bears the faintest evidence of his touch. He could do it. Thale is right there, too close and not close enough.

Zzzing!

Sparks fly up and down his mechanical arm.

"Damn it! She said it was good as new."

Thale retreats out of his hold, and Leon feels unreasonably bereft. He stumbles to catch the edge of the counter. Thale coughs into his hand. The cat meows loudly and happily up at him, and it's like a bubble popping, abrupt and unpleasant as the lull that surrounded Leon dissipates. Logic and sense returning to him, he watches as Thale shuffles from foot to foot, wringing his hands.

"It didn't spark you, did it?"

The man shakes his head. "You okay?"

"I'll be fine. Just a loose cable, most likely."

"I mean, your head."

Leon blinks stupidly before realizing the pain at the back of his head is gone. Rubbing a hand over the area, he notes the knob at the back of head is also missing. Not even tenderness remains in the area.

"How did you—?"

"Just an old trick my mother taught me. Works like a charm." Thale cuts off his question with a hurried answer, a half-smile on his lips. He lets go of the countertop to gesticulate his point and nearly topples over as the ship rocks again.

Thale's clumsiness is even worse onboard. On land, Leon might have assumed it was because the man was more accustomed to being on a boat than on solid ground, lacking "land-legs" as it were, but apparently, his balance is even worse onboard.

"You've never been on a ship before, have you?"

It comes out like a question, but Leon already knows the answer, confirmed when Thale wilts like a damp daisy.

"That obvious, huh?"

Irritation replaces any of the remaining wonder at his miraculously healed head injury.

"Unbelievable... Do you even know how to swim?"

The laugh he receives for that question is bright and cheery.

"I know how to swim very well, Master Leo. I prefer it, actually."

Yeah, he bets. Can't exactly fall when you're in the water.

"Good. The last thing I need to worry about is you drowning yourself if you go overboard."

A soft smile pulls at the mole beside Thale's lip as he looks down and away from Leon.

"Would you dive in after me if I did?"

Long eyelashes unveil ocean deep eyes, a coy gesture if Leon's ever seen one, not unlike the one the man gave him as he wound his legs around Leon's waist the night before. His pants tighten as the memories ghost through his mind.

He doesn't answer Thale's question. There is a secret hidden inside that question he doesn't want to face yet. One that he is not ready to confirm or deny to Thale in the wake of the decision he made that very morning about not dragging this beautiful man into a life on the run. Yet here he is, staring at the object of his affection from the opposite side of the galley, the poor, ignorant beauty having followed Leon here all of his own accord. And Leon suffers no delusions about that. Even if he does have ulterior motives for booking passage on the *C-Devil*, he chose this ship because of Leon. He'd said as much while they'd been bickering at the pier.

So, he leaves, running away from Thale like the cowardly pirate he knows himself to be, and in his retreat, Thale's eyes wash over his back like an ocean tide.

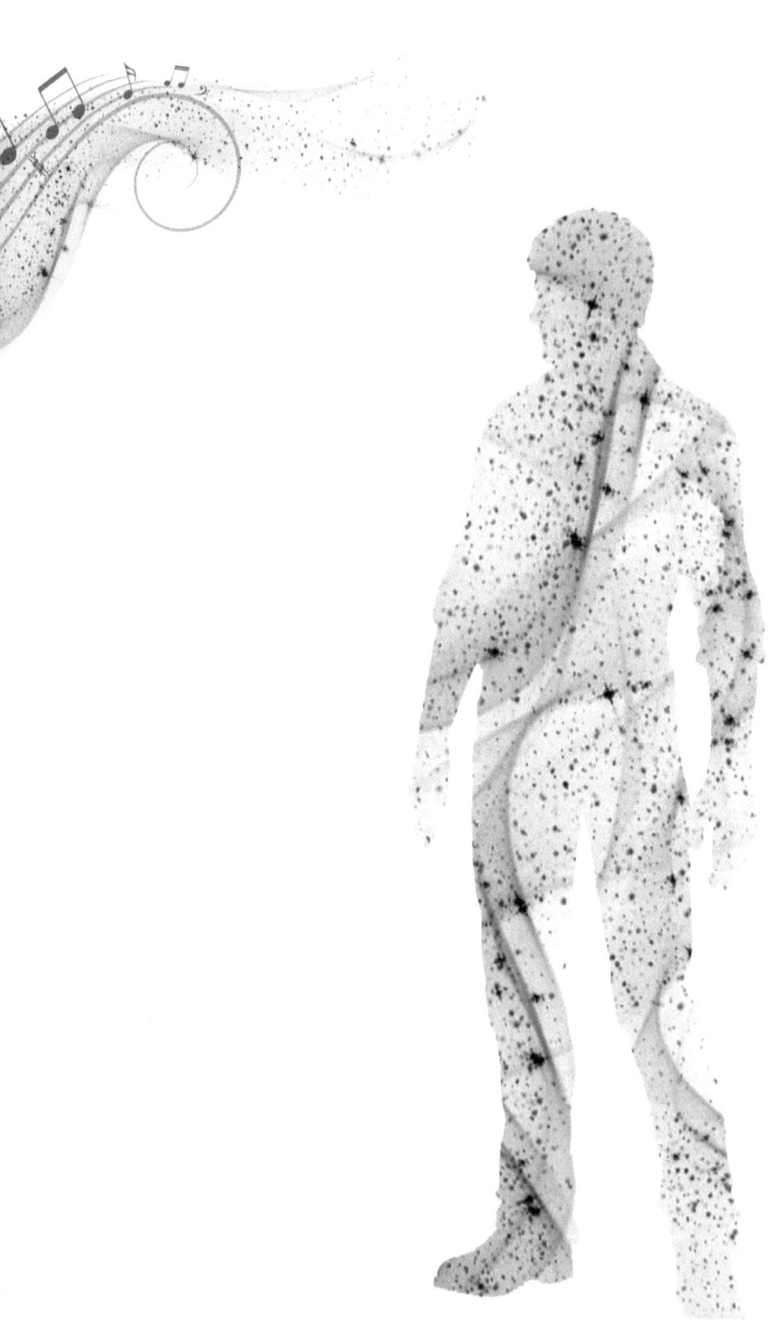

5

Yo Ho, Ho...

LEON WAKES UP TO A POUNDING HEAD-ache behind his eyes, his mouth dry as sawdust. His stomach churns, no doubt looking to punish him for trying to keep up with Izacc and Cassiopeia. He cracks an eye open, sees the too-bright sunlight filtering in through the porthole and nearly vomits when the world around him spins. He screws his eyes shut and groans loudly and miserably. That's when he notices the hand stroking gently across his back.

"Shh... I've got you."

The voice is soft like a lullaby. Even in his misery he recognizes the owner instantly.

"Thale..." he murmurs into the soft warm cushion under his cheek. "What are you...?" He is hushed again. He makes a noise of protest as he feels himself being lifted up and off his nice warm pillow. It's replaced with something cold and far less appealing. The hand at his back presses down.

"Lie still. I'm going to bring you some water."

The sound of bare feet pad away and then nothing but the quiet creaking of the ship until Thale returns. Strong but small hands lift him once more, and he is settled back against the other man's chest. The rim of a drinking vessel is pressed to his lips. He groans at the prospect of drinking anything.

What the hell happened last night?

"Drink slowly."

Leon grips the mug around Thale's hands and does as he's told. When he is finished, a stick of some kind is pressed into his hands.

"Chew on this for a bit. It'll help."

It's a root of some kind. Kind of gummy to close his teeth on, but the taste is somewhere between mint and lemongrass and rather pleasant to be honest. It is also rather effective as he finds the churning in his stomach weakening. The respite is enough for him to realize that he is naked in his cot with Thale. The naked part isn't so much a problem since he usually sleeps nude but with Thale... Top that off with the fact that he has no memory of what he did last night.

"Thale!" he shouts, bolting upright. He immediately regrets it as the water he just drank crawls up his throat.

"I am here."

Those hands coax him back down. One of them plays with his hair. Turning to the man behind him, slower this time and more mindful of his pathetic self, he grips Thale by the shoulders, eyes wide, red-rimmed, and panicked.

"What did I do last night? Did we..."

"Shh... it's alright."

"It's not alright! If I did something, if I—"

*What if I forced myself on Thale? What if—*A finger lines up over his lips.

"Hush. You didn't do anything." The man giggles fondly. "You're very clingy when you're drunk."

Clingy! I am not clingy!

"He lives!"

Izacc's voice is harsh enough that Leon's stomach rolls at the sound of it. Leon's forehead thuds against Thale's chest like a drum, and he swallows around the bile threatening to rise in his throat. Thale just rubs his back some more and coaxes the weird stick thing back between his teeth. He feels like the man is babying him. He doesn't like that he is in a state fit to need babying, but he is not unappreciative of the attention.

"Leon! You're alive," calls Yoshi, bouncing through the hatch. "Though I can see that he's still very much attached to Thale. You two have fun last night?"

Leon doesn't need to see Yoshi's eyebrow waggle to know it's there. He flips the bird his way.

"Get lost, Yoshi."

"Ah, that would be a 'no.' Damn! I knew I should have kept that fourth bottle away from you," announces Izacc. Suddenly, the memories of what he did last night come back to Leon. Taking shots over a game of poker, continuing to drink after they were kicked off the table for getting belligerent, latching onto Thale when his tongue has loosened and his sensibilities were lost to the sea.

He groans, pulling the blanket back over his head.

The pair move in on him. Yoshi tries to yank the sheet off, but Leon grips it tight and holds firm while Izacc proceeds to smack him on the ass.

"Wake up, Leonito! Loupe wants you to help the Habernathy group set nets. You know you're the best at tying knots."

"Keep smacking my ass, and I swear, I will puke all over you."

"That bony thing you call an ass! For shame!" laughs Yoshi. Leon throws a pillow at his head. He feels the rumble of laughter from the chest under his head. It's nice. He curls further into the rolling sound.

"Yuck! Let poor Thale go. He has better things to do than nurse your sorry ass back to adulthood."

Just then Cassiopeia crowds into the small space with a filled bucket of water in hand.

"I've got cold seawater. Tell me if I need to soak 'em."

Water splashes onto Leon's sheets by his feet, and Thale surges upward and out of the bed, clearly not wanting to get a faceful of seawater.

"That would be my cue to go."

"Wait," mumbles Leon as he sinks face first into the bedding. No sooner is Thale out of the splash zone than cold water, as promised by Cassiopeia, is dumped over his head. Leon lurches onto his feet, sputtering and hissing as the saltwater stings his eyes. "I'm awake, you bastards! Now, sod off!"

He at least has the presence of mind to hold the now soaked sheet around his hips lest he embarrass himself further that way, too—not that he has anything to be embarrassed about in that department. He is going to murder his crewmates, slowly and painfully, and when he's done, he'll bring them all back to life so he can do it again. They must sense the murder in his thoughts because all three of them skip their way out of the room.

"See you on deck, Leo. Make sure you get some clothes on first."

The hatch closes, and Leon uses the sheet to dry himself off, not realizing there is still one person in the room.

"Um, I'll just, uh, let myself out."

Leon's eyes fly open to find Thale, pink as a posy, trying desperately not to look at Leon's dripping wet body.

Now, Leon knows what he looks like. Leon's body is a sculpture carved from the palest of sunstones, and the water drips down the planes of his chest and stomach in sinful rivulets. Toned abs, lean muscle, and skin the color of bleached sand from long hours in the sun.

A smirk rises to his lips.

"*Mon haut* is always welcome to watch."

Thale meets his teasing gaze head on. He doesn't flinch, nor does he blush further at the overt invitation. He looks, instead, disheartened by it. He turns away from Leon, moving carefully over the puddle on the floor to the hatch.

"Monsieur Leon shouldn't say things he doesn't mean."

Leon turns away, shamefaced. He does mean it. That's the problem.

Thale's hand closes over the handle and pulls, opening the door as Leon gets his senses back together. He's been behaving like a total ass.

"You're right. I shouldn't have said that."

Thale pauses. Leon wraps the sheet back around his waist, brings his hands together over his heart, and delivers the kind of bow his mother taught him to use when someone important has shown him kindness, a bow that offers respect and gratitude in equal measure alongside a promise to be worthy of the kindness that has been given.

"Thank you for taking care of me, Thale. I'm sorry I caused you trouble last night."

Thale's expression turns soft, a quiet ease in the lines of his lips.

"None at all, Leon. None at all."

The hatch closes behind Thale, and Leon slaps himself in the face. It's the least he deserves anyway.

A few days later, Leon has settled himself atop one of the crates the Habernathy group brought aboard to clean his sniper rifle when Cassiopeia sneaks up on him.

"Pining from afar again, Leo?" Cassiopeia teases him for umpteenth time in the last few days. He's been caught watching Thale again, the man currently helping one of the fishermen pull in some netting. Habernathy curses as once again the net pulls up empty, only a few mackerel and snapper to show for their efforts. Leon still isn't quite sure what exactly they're fishing for, but they leave the nets down most of the day, so to see them reel in this little is more than a bit disturbing.

"You know, if I weren't a lesbian, I'd be on that like a barnacle on a ship. Easy on the eyes, and he has that amazing voice—which by the way he still refuses to share with any of us. I've asked him three times now. He's sweet but feisty and can cook a hell of a lot better than Yoshi. Poseidon below, if he were a woman, I'd have asked him to marry me for the cooking alone."

It's true. Thale has taken to helping Yoshi prepare meals over the last couple of days. It started with him mostly watching the witch work, helping prepare this or that for cooking or baking, but after a while, he'd asked if he could actually prepare the food himself. Yoshi had taken one bite of the fish and rice Thale made and immediately declared himself retired from chef's duties. They'd all been in better spirits for it. Yoshi's food is palatable, but Thale's cooking is something to look forward to.

That's why he's helping with the fishing nets this afternoon, sticking a few choice fish into a bucket for this evening's dinner before tossing the rest back over the rail. He hoists the full bucket in hand and moves toward the hatch that will take him below deck. Thale glances in their direction, and for a split second, and not for the first time since they set sail, Leon feels like he's been stung by a jellyfish. Leon looks away so fast, the long hook and shell earring dangling from his left ear smacks against his cheek. He shakes it back and adjusts his head scarf, quickly going back to his work oiling and swiping the barrel of the rifle.

Cassiopeia, who's been observing the whole exchange, lets out an exaggerated sigh.

"Why do you insist on avoiding him?"

"I'm not avoiding him."

He had just spent the morning helping Thale reorganize the galley. Could he have done that if he was avoiding him? No, and he'll probably be in there again later to help the man bring tonight's meal up to the rest of the crew just like he's been doing the last three days. Had Loupe forced him to help? Yes, but that was beside the point.

"You're avoiding him. If Loupe asks me one more time to come check on you because you've been staring at Thale for too long again, I'm going to scream."

Leon glances up at the helm where the aforementioned captain currently navigates.

"Loupe needs to learn how to leave well enough alone. So do Izacc and Yoshi for that matter."

So, his crewmates are secretly keeping tabs on him. He wouldn't be surprised to find Yoshi keeping a tally of every time he was caught staring at Thale. Hell, he's caught himself staring at the man so often, even he's starting to wonder why he's making a concerted effort to maintain distance and decorum when he can't look away from the beautiful man long enough to get any work done.

Would you dive in after me?

Yes, he would.

Gods, he is so far gone for the man, and being around him the last few days has only made it all the more clear to Leon that what he felt that night in the bar was not a fleeting lust at first sight. It was something more. And now, with Thale integrating himself seamlessly on board, Leon is constantly having to remind himself why he needs to fight against his heart, and honestly, it's starting to wear him down.

"Leon…"

There is a mewing sound from the floor, and Leon turns to find her majesty pawing at his dangling boot. She *brps* at him again before rolling onto her back, paws up, belly exposed, looking up at him sweetly, asking for cuddles.

Thale named the cat Coconut, which is both appropriate, considering how absolutely nutters the animal is toward anyone who isn't Thale, and inappropriate, considering the animal is supposed to be acting as a ratter on a pirate vessel, but hey, who is Leon to judge? He doesn't like the little fluff ball anyway. Well, okay, she let him pet her that one time, and it was nice until she bit him. Why she is presently pawing at his boot is anyone's guess.

"You aren't fooling me again, cat. I remember what happened the last time you tricked me into giving belly rubs."

He has the bite marks to prove it, too. The animal huffs in apparent disappointment.

He shakes his head and makes the mistake of looking up to find Thale smiling at him. The man looks away abruptly when their eyes meet. Leon's mouth quirks up in a lopsided grin. At least he isn't the only one having trouble keeping his eyes to himself.

"See, even the damn cat is telling you not to be so dour."

The expression falls flat off of Leon's face, and Leon is about to show Cassiopeia "dour" when a ruckus goes up across the deck. It's Habernathy's right hand man, Carrow.

"We've got a live haul, fellas! Ericson, get a hold of the line. Smith, I need an extra hand here!"

There is a flurry of activity as the fishermen gather around their equipment. Habernathy plods down from where he was speaking with Loupe at the helm. There is a lot of yelling and general barking of orders among them, and they can't seem to agree on who should be listened to until Habernathy barks at all of them to clean it up. He also calls for the doctor for some unknown reason.

"Hey, Leo, something's up with your man."

Thale stops short just as he is about to duck down into the hatch. The beauty looks confused and more than a little concerned as a large fin is hauled over the lip of the railing.

Leon doesn't respond to Cassiopeia, but he does keep a close eye on Thale who is looking more than a little apprehensively at the net as whatever is trapped inside thrashes wildly, nearly sending three men onto their backs. When they finally manage to haul it onboard, Habernathy curses.

"Drats! I was hoping this was it!"

Flapping and flopping on the deck is one of the largest fish Leon has ever seen. A blue marlin. Approximately eight feet long from the tip of its bill to the end of its tail, the fish is a sight to behold. Any trophy fisherman would crow at the prospect of adding that to his wall. So, why does this group of fishermen seem disappointed with their catch?

"Why did you swim so close to the ship?"

The words are quiet and laced with sorrow. Leon nearly misses Thale's question. It strikes him as a rather odd question to ask. Leon has seen swordfish and sailfish brush right up against the bow before. It isn't unusual. Maybe because Thale doesn't really know much about sailing? But that doesn't seem right either.

"Well, it'll make a handsome trophy, don't you think, cousin?" asks Carrow, coming up to smack Habernathy on the shoulder.

Habernathy wrinkles his nose at the contact. He stands with his cane beside the marlin as it thrashes.

"Please, cousin, I've seen much bigger Marlin than that. Get those nets back in the water. It's bad enough that I mistook that thing for what we're actually looking for. Come on. We're wasting precious minutes."

"Aye! You heard the man, mates. Get that net back in the water."

Two of the men roll the marlin over, its fins folding under itself, to yank out the netting. They unfold it and march back to the railing without giving it a second glance.

"Wait!" shouts Thale as he runs across the deck. "Aren't you going to throw it back?"

Habernathy looks up, stunned, at Thale. It's almost comical how much shorter the businessman is next to Thale's considerable height. He barely comes up to Thale's chest, and he is so round he is twice the width of the thin beauty.

"Why?"

"It's suffocating. If you don't throw it back, it'll drown."

Habernathy, seeming to decide Thale is not a threat, shrugs.

"So, let it drown. It's just a fish. We can use it as bait."

"It's not some mackerel or tuna. Blue marlin are… Look, they're important, and you've already said you don't want it, so throw it back before it dies. Let it return home."

"What are you? Some kind of nutter? Fish don't have homes. They're fish. If you want it tossed back into the water so badly, do it yourself. My men are busy, and I doubt any of these fine gentlemen who have welcomed us aboard their vessel are going to care enough to stop what they are doing to save a stupid fish."

Thale attempts to plead with the man, but he is ignored, a heavily ringed hand dismissing him as the man disappears below deck. Leon frowns at the man's dismissal of Thale, who looks down helplessly at the still twitching swordfish. Leon sets his work down on the crate, ignores Cassiopeia's questioning expression, and strides forward. He sets a hand on Thale's shoulder.

"Thale, it's alright."

"But—"

"I'll help you."

"You will?"

Leon nods, but Thale still looks crestfallen.

"We can't move it with just the two of us."

Leon's hand trails down Thale's back as he nudges him forward.

"Sure, we can. Let me show you what these augmentations can do."

It takes some work to lift the 200lb fish, especially since for the first couple of minutes, the marlin struggles quite violently against them, but eventually, with Leon's augmentations glowing brilliant green with exertion, the tail fin goes over the deck, and the large fish flies nose first into the sea. Leon is a bit worried at how little the animal was fighting back, its tail weakly twitching in his hold while Thale guided its head over the rail. Thale leans against the rail, watching attentively, whispering something under his breath that Leon doesn't quite catch. The more seconds tick by, the more fretful Thale gets. His whole body vibrates with tension until, like a cut string, he sags with despair.

"Dammit!"

Leon searches Thale's face looking for an inkling of what to do. He's not good at this, the whole comfort thing. How do you comfort someone when you aren't entirely sure what they're upset about?

"Thale?"

The man in question sighs, the tiny sound resonant with the waves below.

"It's cruel." Thale's voice is thick as though with unshed tears. "Humans think they can take ownership of anything they find. The human+ are even worse. Even when they find something they don't want, they'll keep it just to watch it die."

"Hey," says Leon, leaning forward and tilting his head sideways. "Not all of us cyborgs are so bad."

A small smile quirks at those lips, and while Leon still isn't entirely sure how this man has the ability to care so much about a fish's death, he is glad, at least, that he was able to get this much from him.

"Ah, yes, sorry. You're right. You're not like that."

"Eh." Leon shrugs. "There are better men than me out there. One of them is standing right next to me."

Thale laughs. It's a mellow sound, not as full of music as normal.

"If you only knew..."

Leon turns his body to look at Thale. With the sun behind him, the beauty's profile is chiseled in shadow, all smooth lines and devastating curves.

"If I only knew what?"

Thale shakes his head.

"Nothing, Monsieur De Mares. Forget I said anything."

Leon resists the temptation to roll his eyes. *Like that's even remotely possible.* Leon couldn't forget anything Thale has said thus far even if somebody shot him in the head. Leon's smirk widens as an idea strikes him.

"Ah, yes, how could I forget? Thale has shown me his wickedness."

The lascivious smirk on his face inspires a blush to rise on Thale's face.

"You speak like this, Leon De Mares?"

Leon continues as though Thale hasn't protested at all.

"A sinful encounter he could never forget. Though really, this humble sailor has been blessed by the heavens to have been allowed to touch such a peerless being."

"Leon..."

Leon presses on.

"Thale is too pure for this world. Too beautiful and so good he tries to help a swordfish find its way home. Nothing could make me change my mind about *mon haut*. Not even if he told me he was a demon himself forever banished from his home and never able to return."

The man's laughter is all the reward Leon needs for that airy performance. Nevermind that he means every word even if the delivery was more akin to that of an overinflated actor than his usual self. Thale calms with a low hum before looking over at Leon.

"Well, I'm not a demon. At least, I don't think I am anyway, and no one can ever banish someone from their home. A true home is always ready to welcome you back, Leon. Even if you think you've lost it forever."

"Ah, he is a poet now. Thale's talents are unending."

"Leon," he admonishes.

"Flowery language does not reality make, *mon haut*."

A warm hand settles over Leon's, and it stuns him into looking straight into Thale's eyes.

"It's true, Leon. Home will always be there waiting for you to find it again."

Somehow, Leon gets the distinct feeling Thale isn't just talking about a physical place.

"Do you know where yours is, *mon haut*?" asks Leon.

Dark irises slide from the horizon to Leon's booted feet. They trace up the line of his body so, so slowly. The intimacy of it is somehow too much and not enough, more poignant than sex, more volatile, yet innocent at once. It leaves him wanting, aching for something he doesn't have the guts to name yet.

"I don't know, Leo. Have you found yours?"

That's when the marlin breaches the surface.

Leon has lived by the sea and on the sea his whole life, and there are fewer sights he can name more awe-inspiring than the sight of that marlin breaching skyward. The fish's deep blue scales flash like sapphires in the sunlight, droplets of water spraying into the air only to cascade back down in misty rainbows.

The tail fin disappears beneath the surface, and Thale beams brighter than the sun. He steps back away from the rail with a nod of triumph. He offers a squeeze to Leon's hand.

"Thank you, Leon. I couldn't have saved him alone."

Thale moves to reclaim his bucket of fish, and before Leon can figure out what he wants to say, the man disappears below deck. For a moment, Leon wants to go after him, but Izacc chooses that exact time to call down from the crow's nest for Leon to take the next shift. He apparently needs to piss.

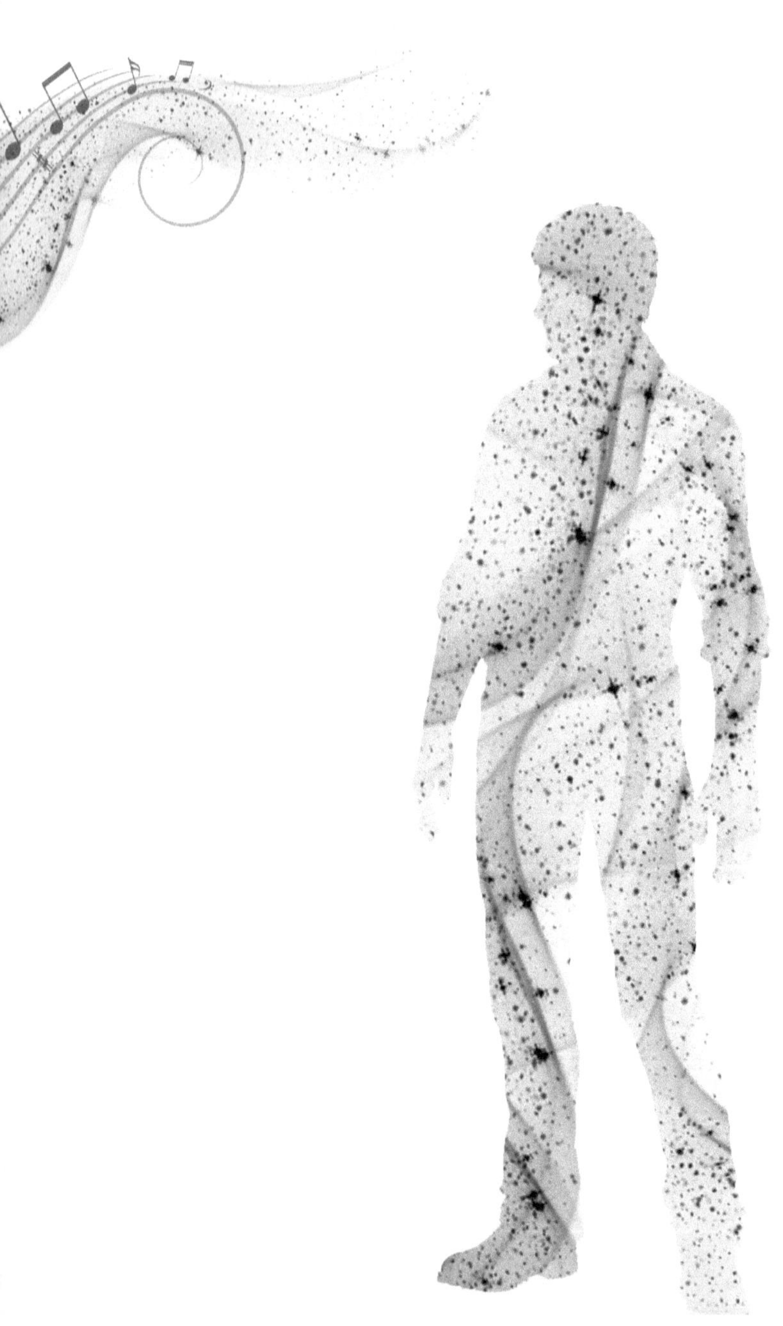

6

...And a Bottle of Rum

THAT NIGHT, CASSIOPEIA DECIDES after dinner that she's bored, so she ventures below deck only to return with her old viola, inspiring Izacc to fish out his guitar. Yoshi flips a barrel sideways to use as a drum, and Loupe grabs some spoons from the galley. One of the fishermen even produces a harmonica to join in. Other than that, most of Habernathy's crew keep to themselves, arm wrestling and playing cards while they enjoy the music.

Leon sits just outside of the circle of men, tapping his foot and offering his voice every so often against Loupe's singing. He isn't drinking tonight. He hasn't drunk much at all really after having the piss taken out of him by his oh-so-loving crewmates for, apparently, dragging Thale around the deck that first night at sea.

It had been embarrassing to hear secondhand about his behavior. Talking nonsense about being handed a treasure map and needing to take better care of the treasure now that it had walked onboard with him. Musing aloud about how he was going to keep said treasure from drowning to death the moment something went wrong. He tried to feed the man noodles, climb him like a tree, and take the man swimming only to be rejected at each turn. He'd even whined quite pitifully while propositioning Thale for a repeat performance of that oh-so memorable drone ride. And no matter what anyone did, he flat out refused to go to bed until Thale himself volunteered to look after him, humming something that sounded suspiciously like a lullaby to get him to calm down.

The next day, a few members of Habernathy's group looked at him like he was a total nut.

So, he sits and sips at the one goblet of rum he is allowing himself for the evening and claps his hands as Yoshi finishes singing some ballad about a fishmonger's daughter. The song ends with a crash of notes, and Yoshi skips over to him looking far too excited for Leon's sense of self-preservation.

"Leon, you should dance next."

And that is a horrible idea. "Nah, Yoshi."

"Aw come on!" Yoshi's pitch lowers as he speaks behind his hand in a faux whisper. "I bet if you show off a little, Thale will notice."

"Oh, yes!" laughs Izacc, coming up as well. "Show him how Leon De Mares really gets the boat rocking."

"I was under the impression he already had."

Leon chucks a piece of bread at Loupe before glancing in Thale's direction.

Thale sits quietly just a few feet away from Leon among a pile of rope and netting. He's lying down on his side more than sitting, an old ledger he found in the galley laid on the floor in front of him, and he appears to be sketching something, a piece of charcoal in one hand scraping across the paper.

As though he can sense he is being spoken of, Thale looks up from his work. He seems curious about what it is they are discussing, and Leon has the sudden urge to hear Thale sing. Thus far, Thale has been content to hum along with Loupe and Yoshi's vocals. Leon has been listening to that humming all evening from across the deck. It's dreamy and smooth, and it reminds Leon of days long gone, and Leon wants to hear the full quality of that voice so he can stop being driven mad by the barely there sound of it. Cassiopeia has already tried to get Thale to sing only to be rebuked despite the best set of puppy dog eyes she could muster.

Leon has a feeling he'll be luckier.

"I'll dance if Thale sings a song for us." He says it loud enough for Thale to hear, and sure enough, Thale's left eyebrow lifts.

"Oh? Monsieur De Mares wishes to hear this one sing?"

"This monsieur would very much like to hear his *mon haut* sing."

It's too dark for Leon to see Thale's blush in the lantern light, but he hears it in his voice.

"I'm not that good, really," he protests with a laugh.

"Impossible!" declares Izacc. "We've all heard you hum."

Leon gets up from his place and strides over to the flustered male.

"Come on, Thale. Let me hear you sing," he challenges, and the words drip with innuendo.

"Leon De Mares!"

Leon smiles cheekily and more than a little flirtatiously at the older man. Catching on, Yoshi begins a chant of Thale's name, the rest of the crew, even the fishermen, chiming in wholeheartedly.

"Thale, Thale, Thale..."

At last the man caves, but Leon isn't sure if it is the chanting that does him in or the way Leon openly gazes at him.

"Alright, alright, but don't get mad when it's terrible."

"Nonsense! Here, let me accompany you," says Cassiopeia, gesturing with her instrument. "I can follow pretty well. Just give me a key to work in.

Thale sets his makeshift sketchbook aside and folds his legs underneath him as he sits up. He hums a few notes so Cassiopeia can pick up the key signature and then, without any fanfare, starts a familiar sea shanty Leon has heard a few times in various bars but never has he heard it sung quite so hauntingly.

Upon one summer's morning,
I carefully did stray
Down by the docks of Mont Hav
Where I met a sailor gay.

His hair it hangs in ringlets,
His eyes they glow like coal,
My happiness attend him
Wherever he may go.

From Deriva's shores to Tai Tides
I'll wander, weep, and moan
All for my jolly sailor
Until he sails home.

My heart is pierced by Cupid.
I disdain all glittering gold.
There is nothing can console me,
But my jolly sailor bold.

My sailor is as smiling
As the pleasant Month of Rain,
And often we have wandered
From o'er the ocean far.

Come all you pretty fair maids
Whoever you may be
Who love a jolly sailor
That plows the raging sea

While up aloft in storm
From me his absence mourn
And firmly pray arrive the day
He's never more to roam

My heart is pierced by Cupid.
I disdain all glittering gold.
There is nothing can console me
But my jolly sailor bold.

As the last note falls, a total hush falls over them like a veil. Leon's mates, who were toasting their success in finally getting Thale to sing, have all but dropped their bottles of rum in astonishment. Cassiopeia, mesmerized by the magic of his voice, stopped playing halfway through Thale's song. Even the fishing crew stopped to listen.

Leon finds that he has drifted closer to Thale, now sitting next to him rather than halfway across the deck. He has no idea when he moved, and he doesn't care. He feels like he is seeing Thale for the first time. Time stretches between them, inconsequential, as he holds Thale's gaze, the song-spell tying them together as firmly as any sail line. The lantern lights glimmer in Thale's deep irises. The same is mirrored in Leon's own dark, midnight gaze.

He doesn't know if he'll ever have the strength to look away again.

The sudden splashing sound of a fish breaking the water's surface off the prow tears the gossamer thread holding everyone's breath hostage. Loupe is the first one to clap, and he is quickly joined by the rest of the men—Leon included.

"That was amazing."

Thale looks away, and Leon ducks down to recapture those eyes.

"You should move back, Leon De Mares."

"Only if you promise to sing for me again."

"That's very dangerous."

Leon's eyebrow lifts. That's not the response he was expecting.

"How so?"

Thale opens his mouth to answer and then closes it, his lips looking all the more soft and enticing as he waffles for an answer. He chews on his lower lip, teeth tugging at the mole there, and why should Leon resist the sudden desire to drag the man below deck, again?

"That performance deserves a drink, if I've ever heard one!"

Loupe's voice brings Leon further back to himself, and he realizes just how close he is to Thale, inappropriately close, nearly crowding the man against the crates behind him. He only moves back to check where his captain is. Loupe is making his way over, a bottle of rum in hand.

"What do you say, Thale? Fancy a bit of a swig before you give us an encore?"

Thale startles.

"Encore?"

"Too right, you bloody blighter," shouts Cassiopeia. "You've been holding out on us, keeping that voice to yourself while these sorry sods sing us into an early grave."

Yoshi and Loupe both glare at the woman, but several members of Habernathy's group agree with loud resounding "Hear-Hears!" and Habernathy himself even claims he'll pay good money to hear Thale sing again. Thale waves his hands in front of him in protest.

"I'm really not that good."

Thale shuffles backward, inadvertently backing up into Leon's chest. When Leon wraps his arms around him to keep him toppling over, he feels Thale's body temperature noticeably rise.

"Fibber," Leon whispers into Thale's ear before setting the man firmly on his feet. He then sways away into the circle of lantern light, boasting louder. "Come on, Thale. If you sing for me, I'll dance for you."

"Wh—Who wants you to dance for them, anyway?" Thale sputters, and Leon grins in response.

"I'm the best dancer on the seven seas. Who doesn't want to see me dance?"

Thale's eyes narrow as he laughs. "Your pride is showing."

"Your stubbornness is showing," he shoots back.

"I'm stubborn?"

"Hm." Leon nods. "Your very presence here is case and point to that."

Thale gapes at him like a fish. Yoshi spits up the mouthful of rum in laughter. Loupe rolls his eyes and takes a swig from the bottle.

"Don't listen to him."

"No, no, listen to him. I want to hear Thale sing again," protests Yoshi.

"Just one more," pleads Cassiopeia.

Peer pressure is a terrible thing, and they are all wretches for turning their begging on Thale collectively, but when it works, it works. Thale takes the bottle of rum from Loupe and upends it over his open mouth. Leon watches hungrily as Thale's throat works to drink down the liquid. Four gulps of alcohol, and Thale pulls the bottle away with a shudder and a cough.

"Oh, it's a party now," Carrow crows from where he sits watching Thale. Izacc whoops and then pushes Thale into their circle.

"What are we playing, Maestro?"

Thale laughs, voice already thick with alcohol.

"Do you know 'Laughter in the Deep'?"

Cassiopeia laughs and starts to play.

It isn't just one more song. Nor is it one dance, and the spirits flow heartily around the deck. The hour grows late, and before long, Thale is a flushed, giggly mess swaying about the deck. And this is more than a little surprising because Thale really didn't drink much more than a few mouthfuls.

"You really are a lightweight."

Leon tugs Thale into his lap before the man can tumble to the floor from all of the spinning he's been doing. Yoshi had challenged him to a spin off and in his intoxicated state Thale agreed. He'd miraculously won the spin off, but it doesn't seem to be by very much.

"I'm fine, Leo," he slurs and then promptly drops his head onto Leon's chest.

"Mhmm, yeah, I believe you."

Izacc laughs. "Poor guy. No wonder he didn't want to drink. Captain, you are a cruel, cruel man, making one of our guests drink."

Loupe, head cocked to the side, replies, "How was I to know? And besides, he is the one who accepted the drink."

Leon's soul nearly leaves his body as Thale throws his legs on either side of his hips and nuzzles his face into Leon's collarbone. Guess Leon isn't the only one who gets clingy when drunk.

"You know, my mother always said 'never to go dancing with sailors.'"

Thale's speech is slurred and musical like he's recounting a fond memory. The man giggles, grinding down unintentionally on Leon's building arousal. Leon holds him by the waist to prevent him from moving any farther.

"Thale!"

"Human tales..." He hiccups, closing his eyes and resting against Leon's shoulder. *Gods, how is he so adorable?*

"Leon, why don't you take Thale down? I think he's done."

Leon laughs as he carries the inebriated Thale down to the galley where he's been sleeping the last few nights. There is a hammock set up between two pillars, and Leon carefully settles him in the fabric. Thale mumbles in protest as he pulls away.

"What am I going to do with you?"

"Keep me."

Thale's eyes are open, hazy and alcohol soaked but open and mildly alert. Leon feels caught like a fish hiding from a shark. But Thale doesn't maintain that level of wakefulness very long, eyelids falling heavy over his eyes.

"You can always keep me."

The sentence is punctuated by a barely audible snore. Leon laughs quietly.

"You're a right terror, you know that." The fondest of admonitions given as he brushes the hair out of the man's face.

Leon removes the man's boots, refrains from lingering too long over the shape of those thin ankles, and looks around for a blanket to throw over Thale but finds nothing. *Has he been sleeping uncovered?* He's lucky he hasn't caught anything yet.

Leon leaves the man where he lies and goes to his own quarters. He has a spare. He can't have their current cook catching his own death, can he?

It takes him a few minutes to scavenge for the damned thing—it was hanging out in Yoshi's mess of a clothes chest—but find it he does. If he returns to the galley with a slight hop to his step, it's certainly more to do with that than the prospect of properly tucking in a sleeping beauty.

When he makes it back, the galley door is shut. Odd, he doesn't remember closing it. He twists the knob and finds it locked. He certainly hadn't locked it either, and Thale had been in no state to get up and do it himself.

"Get off..."

Thale's slurred protest is muffled but just loud enough to hear through the door. Leon's eyes widen, the sounds of struggle now audible through the door.

Leon grits his teeth and shoves his augmented shoulder hard into the jamb. The door swings open with a bang, splinters scattering in the air.

Rage nearly blinds him at what he finds on the other end.

7

The Eye of the Storm

HABERNATHY'S MAN, CARROW, hovers over Thale on the floor, one hand around his throat, the other pawing into Thale's top, now falling off his shoulder. Upon Leon's entrance, the bastard pushes Thale facedown hard.

Leon closes the distance in a heartbeat and punches the man square in the jaw. The hit throws Carrow across the galley and into two bags of flour. The brute coughs and laughs as he pats the flour from his clothes and face, not yet looking at Leon.

"Nice punch, brat! Now fuck off, will you! Whores are meant for sharing, and from what I understand, you've had your turn."

Leon draws his pistol and aims it at the man's head.

"There aren't any whores on this ship."

Carrow raises his hands in front of him.

"Whoa, whoa, easy there, mate. It's just good fun. I weren't gonna do nothing bad to 'em."

Carrow moves to get up, but Leon cocks the hammer of his gun.

"I suggest you stay right there, mate."

He looks to Thale who has crawled backward on his hands to put his back against the wall. He is still kind of out of it from the alcohol, head swaying a little and eyes dilated, but sobriety creeps in fast under an adrenaline surge.

"Thale?"

Thale doesn't answer his call. He doesn't even look at Leon, his focus utter steel as he stares at the man who attacked him. A chill goes down Leon's spine at that look, unfeeling and calculating like a shark's hollow gaze before it strikes.

"Thale!"

The man blinks, and the strange look in his eye dissipates. He blinks again, and it is like he is just now realizing that Leon is in the room.

"Leon?"

"I'm here."

Thale closes his eyes and leans his head back against the wall. He curls into himself, exposing the side of his neck to Leon. He sees the imprint of Carrow's hand already bruising around his throat. Leon's eyes dart toward Carrow, and he fires a single shot directly into the man's hand. Thale startles. The man curses loud enough to reach the main deck as he clenches his hand by the wrist.

"What the fuck! You bloody poof!"

Leon kicks the man in the chest and then swings out a fist, nailing Carrow in the back of his plated head hard enough to knock him into oblivion. Leon holsters his pistol and kneels in front of Thale.

"Thale," he calls, and Thale's eyes barely slide open to look at him. His eyelids look heavy like keeping them open is a chore. The alcohol in his system is no doubt fighting to shut him down while the adrenaline works to keep him awake.

"I'm fine, Leo." His voice is harsh, his vocal cords nearly crushed in the assault. Leon reaches a hand forward, and much to his surprise, Thale leans his head down to nuzzle into his palm. The slighter man sighs. Leon's palm is big enough to cover the whole half of his face. They stay like that for a pulse, and then Thale rasps out:

"He's done it before, you know. He'll do it again next chance he gets."

The iciest sensation drags through Leon's sensorium. *Of course,* he thinks. *Men like that can't wait until they are given something, so they seek to take it by force.*

"I'll be back. Don't go anywhere. I need to take out the trash."

He waits until Thale nods in understanding before extracting himself to deal with the scum on their ship. Just as he expected, Loupe and Izacc are already heading to the galley as he drags the dirtbag outside. Habernathy is hot on their heels, looking for all the world like a frightened chicken.

"Leon, what's happened?"

"This sodding pile of rubbish just attacked Thale."

"What?" declares Loupe.

"You heard me," growls Leon.

"Habernathy, anything to say for your man?"

"W-Well, this is preposterous. Why would Carrow try to kill a man who's done nothing to him?"

"He was trying to rape him," spits Leon.

Habernathy turns green around the gills, and the discussion ends with Carrow being tossed into one of the rarely used holding cells in the brig.

True to his word, Leon returns to the galley after locking the cell himself, handing the key to Izacc. Thale has already picked himself back up and resettled in the hammock. He starts when Leon enters.

"It's me."

Leon lowers the flame on a nearby lantern as he peels off his boots. He pads his way over to Thale, who lifts his head as he approaches.

"Leon?"

"Mm."

"What are you doing?"

Thale trembles, whether from the cool night air or from the dregs of adrenaline and alcohol in his system, Leon doesn't know. Regardless, Leon doesn't answer, not verbally at least. He merely pulls himself up and into the hammock with Thale, pulling the sheet over them as he nestles Thale into his chest.

"Leon, what are you doing?"

"What does it look like? I'm sleeping with you."

"You don't have to do that. I'm not some fair maiden whose virtue needs protecting."

"That ship certainly sailed a while back."

Thale gives him the most exasperated look he thinks he's ever seen on the man. Leon's lips pull up at the edges, and he brushes the hair out of Thale's eyes.

"Go to sleep, Thale. I'm here because I want to be."

Leon then curls farther around the taller man and closes his eyes in faux sleep. He stays awake, mindful of Thale resettling himself in the hammock with a sigh. Eventually, the slighter man's body relaxes against him, and Leon opens his eyes. Eyelashes settled across his cheeks and breathing even, Thale is more than settled, comfortably asleep in Leon's arms.

Leon falls asleep to the sound of Thale's breathing that night.

Leon wakes to the ship surging up beneath him so violently he is thrown from the hammock. He lands in a rumpled pile on the floor with an *oof*, shaking himself to realize he is alone. Where is Thale?

"All hands on deck! All hands on deck!"

Another shudder rips through the ship, and Leon shuffles crablike to stay on his feet before racing toward the main deck. He nearly barrels right into Yoshi who is hopping from one foot to the other trying to pull on his pants.

"What's happening?"

"Cap'n said a huge storm just hit out of nowhere. We aren't even completely upon it yet, and already the sails are threatening to capsize us."

They emerge out of the hatch into a violent windburst that sends the two of them rolling head over heels into the rail.

"Come on, gents!" shouts Loupe from where he is fighting with a line. "Get those sails tied up before we lose the main mast to this bloody wind."

Leon bolts for the main mast to help Cassiopeia, Izacc, and a few of the fishermen get it tied off. He climbs up and anchors himself to the netted ropes next to Cassiopeia by tangling his feet through the lines. He gets a hold of the line and pulls, grinding his teeth.

He scans the deck as he does. There is no sign of his bed-mate anywhere onboard.

"Where's Thale? Have you seen him?"

"Aye," answers Cassiopeia. "He was up here before any of us were rightfully awake. Your boy was the one who spotted the storm clouds. He woke up Loupe who woke up everybody else before it started to get really rough. Gave us at least a thirty-minute head start. We'd already be sunk if he hadn't pointed it out."

"Where is he now?"

"I think he ducked below to find that crazy cat of his just before you and Yoshi made it up. Then there was something about securing the stores in the galley. I ain't seen him since."

"Well, he wasn't in the galley."

"He's down there somewhere, mate. Probably looking for that blasted animal."

A surge of water splashes up onto the deck, sending several crates skidding across the deck.

"Somebody secure that cargo!"

Leon, Cassiopeia, Izacc, and Yoshi manage to wrestle the main sail into folding, and Leon slides on his belly, tying it off while his mates move onto the next mast. It is as he is tying off the last bracer that the sky opens up. *Sea Gods!* He can hardly tell the difference between being in the water and being on the ship by how much water spills from the heavens.

Leon swings down from the mast to land on deck as another wave strikes the bow, knocking Habernathy, who was trying to wrestle a tarp around his precious tank alone, clean over. The man rolls clean off the edge of the railing and into the sea. Leon sees him splash into the water.

"Help! I can't swim!"

"Leon, can you get to him?" calls Cassiopeia.

"On it!"

Leon dives headfirst into the water, swimming his way to Habernathy just as the man's head goes below the water. Leon takes a deep breath and dives. Under the waves, the water is much easier to swim through, and he gets a firm hold under Habernathy's armpits before kicking his way upward. At the surface, he presses the release latch on his arm and a grappling hook shoots toward the ship. Yoshi catches the line.

"Pull!"

"Pull!" echoes Yoshi, and Leon is tugged out of the water, a choking and sputtering Habernathy in his grip. Holy hell is the man heavy. Leon all but throws the man on deck before tying him down to the mast.

"Stay there!"

"But!"

"Stay!" he snarls at the businessman. They have better things to do than babysit a sea slug. Just then a horrible *shinnng!* sound screeches through the pounding rain, and the *C-Devil* jerks beneath their feet, sending all of them tumbling to the deck.

"What was that?" asks one of the fishermen.

"I think we hit a reef," answers Izacc. "Loupe!"

"Leon, take the helm! Izacc, Cassi, get everyone tied down. I'll go below and check it out. Keep everyone's head above water."

Leon De Mares races up to keep the wheel from spinning out of control, lest they go careening toward their deaths while Loupe disappears below. It takes both Leon's synthetic strength and Yoshi's magical force to keep the helm still as the storm worsens.

Leon grits his teeth, closes his eyes, and prays.

It feels like eons pass before the storm's rage calms. Leon feels waterlogged and drowned. His muscles are heavy as lead as he unties the safety cabling around his waist. Loupe calls for a headcount, Izacc offers him some water, and Leon guzzles it down like a lifegiving ambrosia.

"Fuck, that was a mean typhoon. And we only got the outskirts of it. Give your beau a kiss from me for watching the damned horizon while the rest of us whiled away the night like a bunch of lazy louts."

Leon chuckles for a moment before he realizes that Thale is still unaccounted for.

Through the entirety of the storm, Leon never once saw Thale set foot on deck. Leon checks everywhere, the galley, the crew's quarters, the brig, even the loo, and there is no sign of Thale or even Coconut anywhere.

"Loupe, where is Thale?" Leon asks back on the main deck, knowing Loupe was conducting a head count not ten minutes before.

Loupe looks around surprised. "Below deck, I guess. Why?"

"I can't find him anywhere."

"Well, I never saw him up here during the storm, so he can't have gone overboard. Though I didn't see him down there when I sealed the hull either."

"You sealed the hull?"

"Yeah, we were taking on water through a blown board. It should be fine for now. We can repair it at the next port."

"Loupe!"

"What?" Loupe turns wide eyes on Leon.

"You sealed the hull!" Leon takes off running, completely ignoring Loupe's dazed expression.

The hull where Coconut, despite the fact that she has yet to catch anything, likes to go hunting for mice, and where Thale probably went to fetch her during the storm. But Loupe sealed the door hours ago which means that portion of the hull would be completely flooded by now. If Thale was in there when it was sealed, if Loupe didn't realize he was down there, there's no way he could still be alive.

Sure enough, Leon finds the dividing door sealed shut, and he sinks to his knees, seeing the way water has spilled through the cracks to dampen the floorboards. There'll be no way to open it until they've docked to repair the damage. He doesn't have to wonder the fate of anyone who may have been caught on the other side.

He clenches his fists and is about to punch the floor when, *BANG, BANG, BANG*, something hits the inside of the latch head. Was something drifting around in the water? The pattern repeats, and Leon shakes himself.

"Can someone open the door!?"

Impossible...

Leon blinks, struck dumb momentarily before the banging repeats again. Then he is up and moving to open the hatch.

"Mrrow!!!"

Where he expects a rush of water to pour out, he instead receives a very wet, very angry munchkin cat as Coconut zooms through the narrow opening and toward the markedly dryer parts of the ship. The door opens farther, and Thale steps out. The man is barely even damp.

The man's lips quirk up on one side, and he has the nerve to look embarrassed as he scratches the back of his neck.

"Leon! Thanks. I was afraid we would be down there for—"

Leon cuts Thale off, fists clenching into the fabric of the man's collar as he rams Thale into the nearby wall.

"Ow! What the hell, Leon!"

Leon is furious.

"Are you stupid! Running into a breached part of the ship to rescue an ill-tempered cat! Loupe didn't even know you were down here. He locked you inside a coffin, and you don't even realize it."

"Leon—"

"Shut up! You don't get to justify yourself. You could have drowned! I knew I shouldn't have let you step even one foot on board. Do you think this is a game? Is that why you decided to follow me out of Calypso City? We had one good night together, and you think that gives you the go ahead to tag along like a lovestruck fish wife. You don't know any-thing about me. You don't know anything about sailing. You don't know anything about this lifestyle. What were you even thinking coming aboard a pirate ship?"

Leon gives one last shove to Thale's shoulders before backing away. He runs his hands through his hair as his brain catches up to his mouth. He sighs and tries again at a more reasonable volume.

"Thale—"

"You've made yourself very clear," Thale cuts him off, voice carefully measured. Leon whirls around to look at him only to find Thale refusing to meet his gaze. "This one apol-ogizes for offending him and assures him that he'll be rid of this one's presence upon our next arrival to port."

Leon winces as Thale turns to walk away. The finality of it drives him into a panic.

"Thale, wait!" he shouts, catching the man's hand.

Thale halts so quickly he completely loses his balance. Leon lunges forward to steady him, catching him around the biceps. Thale jerks away as though burned.

"What?" he snaps at Leon.

Leon backs up to a respectable distance as a knot forms in his throat; Leon grits his teeth and speaks through it anyway.

"I'm sorry. That's not what I meant. Don't leave. I just..."

"You just what? Can't handle me being here because I was just supposed to be a—what's the term again?—a notch on your bedpost. I'm sorry my presence is such an inconvenience for you. I should have realized. You must leave hand-woven trinkets for all of your conquests," he snarls, flashing the red bracelet still tied onto his wrist where Leon left it before disappearing the morning after their tryst.

"I do not," Leon protests.

"Oh? I must have been a really good lay then."

Thale's dismissal comes with another turn of his head as he makes to leave. That's not it. That's not it at all, and it's not like this is the first time Leon has had to work with a one night stand after the fact, but Thale was never just a one-night stand, was he? Leon grinds his teeth together, clenching his fist, and nearly bursts when the confession spills from his mouth like a bomb.

"I was scared, okay!"

Thale stops and stares back at him stunned.

"But—"

Leon cuts him off before he can fully voice whatever question he was planning to ask.

"The moment I saw you in the bar, I knew. I-I've never connected to someone the way I've connected to you. I've never... I've never felt like this about anyone, and it frightens me." Leon snorts. "Gods, I've never been so frightened of something my entire life. I thought you were dead just now, and I've never felt so out of control in my whole life."

Leon leans sideways into the wall, his hands wringing at his face and hair. He screws his eyes shut and prays for something—he has no idea what but something—to make this easier.

The silence stretches between them, and Leon risks opening an eye to peer over at Thale. The other male is worrying at his lip, seemingly mulling over this information. Maybe this is how Thale finally comes to understand that Leon is a total nutcase who, despite every bad thing that has ever happened to him, still believes in love at first sight. Maybe he will figure out that Leon is a walking bad omen and will make the right decision to avoid any further association between them. Maybe Thale is deciding that he doesn't care that much and will indeed disembark at the next port. It would be better that way. Leon knows that to his very marrow. He just doesn't know if he would survive it.

"Why does it scare you?" Thale's voice is closer, somewhere to his right. The steely tone that was there before is gentler.

"I'm a pirate."

There is a lot to unload in that statement. Leon has seen things, horrible things. Cut out the close calls with nature and the law and other pirates, and still there is a perilous ugliness in this lifestyle that cannot be denied. Men who pillage and take what is not on offer. Others who try and hold on to something only to destroy it whether intentionally or not. Lovers cast out to sea to die together. Cursed love stories that only end in tears.

"I've killed people, I've ruined lives, I've lied and cheated and stolen, and I will keep doing so time and time again so long as the world continues to turn. I'm not some handsome prince or tragic hero that you can sail into the sunset with. I'm a servant of *santa muerte*, a cold-blooded *vato*, and a heartless *tibron*. I'll end up dragging you to hell with me, and I'll laugh about it the whole way down. That's the kind of greedy *fripouille* I am. Che! Look what almost happened today because of a fucking typhoon."

"I don't think the weather has anything to do with you being a pirate."

"That's not the point! The point is you don't deserve to live your life cursed."

Thale laughs.

"You think that's funny?"

"Aye, Leonito, what am I going to do with you?"

Excuse him!

Something on Leon's face must be absolutely fucking hilarious because when Thale meets his eye, he laughs harder. It's melodious and full, similar to how he laughs when he's playing with Coconut. Similar to how he laughed that night at the bar when Leon dragged him out dancing only for him to trip over his own feet; similar to how he laughs with Leon whenever the pirate forgets himself enough to let him in.

"Why are you laughing? This is serious."

"I know. I know, Lee. I'm sorry, it's just... I suffer no delusions about what or who you are." Thale's smaller hands link themselves into his as best as they can. "I know you don't know very much about me yet, and I want to change that, but I'll be brutally honest with you. It scared me, too, falling in love with you."

"Thale," Leon starts, but Thale shakes his head.

"Just let me finish, okay? Then you can say or do whatever you want, but it's my turn, alright?"

Leon nods.

"All my life I have been scared of being trapped and caged, of having my freedom taken away from me, and I was always taught that falling in love was a surefire way to forcibly shackle yourself, chaining yourself down until you drown in your own tears and forget you were ever your own person. They said it's worse when the person you love doesn't love you back. That I could die of a broken heart if I ever let myself go like that. So, I swore that I would never fall in love and be imprisoned by my own heart."

Thale's eyes soften as they gaze down at Leon.

"But then I met you. I met you, and it happened anyway. I've never believed in love at first sight, but it happened, and the feel of it is so incredible that I thought maybe it wouldn't be so bad to bond with someone, to let myself love someone so long as that someone was you. I decided that I would take the risk, and here I am, being yelled at by a bratty pirate for worrying him so much he couldn't keep himself from lashing out because apparently the thought of me drowning to death is too horrible for him to bear. Believe you me, if that is the curse I must bear for loving you, hehe..." He trails off, leaving the sentence unfinished. "There are far worse curses to suffer, Leon."

Thale's expression is the softest that Leon has ever seen as though he is truly touched by Leon's near violent overreaction to the situation. Those warm eyes wash over him, seeing him as though Leon is not a murderer, like he is just a man—a man trying to find his way in this world. The gaze is heavy on Leon's heart, and as the man lifts a hand to caress Leon's face, it flutters like a baby bird trying to fly right out of his chest.

"I know I don't know you, Leon De Mares. I know there are a lot of things about you I will probably never know, and there are also a lot of things you don't know about me, but... I'd like to share them with you one day if you'd have them. I think you're the only man in the whole world I would be willing to share them with."

Leon surges upward, lining them up hip to hip as he finally, finally stops fighting himself and kisses Thale, his odd, beautiful, steadfast soulmate, who he feels he has known for years rather than mere days. *How did we get to this point?* Leon's tears stream down his face as he tries to consume this man who somehow deems him worthy, not just as a onetime lover but as a partner, someone to walk toward the future with, a lifelong companion.

Thale's eyes are closed by the time he pulls away from their kiss, lips swollen and pink, nearly bruised from the ferocity of Leon's desire. Leon tucks his face into Thale's neck and brushes his nose into the collar of Thale's robe.

"I'm sorry, Thale."

Thale coaxes his head up, sweeping away his tears with cool fingertips. He swipes his lips against Leon's in a chaste meeting before ducking into a peck that immediately makes Leon smile.

"I know. It's okay. I know you didn't mean it. Not that part anyway." Thale's eyes sparkle even in the staunch darkness of the belly of the ship. He toys with a button on Leon's coat, spinning it between his fingertips before pressing his palm flat against Leon's chest, right over his pulse. He looks up at Leon through his lashes. How he manages that despite his superior height Leon can't even begin to understand, but he does. "You know, in hindsight, it's kind of cute."

Leon's eyes narrow, the heat in them a far cry from the earlier anger.

"I'll show you cute."

He guides the laughing Thale against the wall. Thale's hands come up to his shoulders, but Leon grasps his wrists one in each hand before pressing them against the wall above his head. Thale's laughter is cut short by Leon's possessive kiss, his tongue snaking its way into the taller man's mouth as he shifts Thale's dainty wrists into one hand, holding them there. Long black hair cascades over Thale shoulders as he throws his head back, putting on display the angry bruises still marring the golden flesh there. Leon nips and bites his way down the long column of his throat, determined to erase those marks, covering them up with his own.

"Mercy! Mercy! You're too much for me, Leon."

"Only if you'll promise me one thing," whispers Leon into thin collarbones. He should've know the taller male would be ticklish.

"Anything."

"Be mine. Forever, be mine."

Thale stops squirming and looks down at him with too-wide eyes. "You have me, Leon. You've had me since the day we met."

"Heh, what pirate in his right mind would say 'no' to treasure when it's right in front of him?"

Thale raises a pointer finger to his chin, looking up at the ceiling in flirty contemplation.

"Hmm, I can think of a pretty stubborn one actually."

He gives Leon the side eye.

"Well, even fools can see the error of their ways."

He cuts off Thale's laughter with his lips fully intending to make this reconciliation count as he slides his hands into Thale's robes.

"Leon! Did you find Thale?"

They startle, Leon barely getting Thale's hanfu back in order before his captain rounds the corner.

"Yes! He's fine," he snips, tugging Thale's collar back together to hide the marks he just finished leaving there.

The man *tsks*, looking the two of them up and down before breaking out in a hearty laugh. Thale's blush is incriminating. Thale steps into Leon's vicinity to whisper that he is going to check on the galley and Coconut before walking away.

"Well, I suppose he is fine, isn't he?" laughs Loupe.

He rounds on Loupe. "No thanks to you. You locked both him and Coconut in the hull for no reason. It didn't even flood."

Loupe frowns at that.

"That's not possible. I saw the water seeping in."

"See for yourself then."

Loupe frowns before striding past, Leon following on his heels. Leon stops at the hatch and gapes at the state of the hull. Everything is tossed about as though there was indeed a flood. Even the ceiling is damp. However, the only water to be found is but a few inches deep.

Leon wanders over to where Loupe remembers the breach occurring. There is indeed a break in the hull, but no water is presently leaking in. He ducks his head underwater and finds the hole clogged up with barnacles, seaweed, and a strange inky, goo-like material.

The day is spent making repairs to the ship. Loupe, seeing the clogged-up break, decides it's best to leave it be until they reach port. He doesn't question it—just lights some incense and offers some fresh fruit to the sea for her mercy. Curiosity is for inviting trouble. Gratitude is for knowing they will not sink anytime soon.

What's more curious is the death of the imprisoned Carrow. Habernathy is up in arms about it, accusing one of the crew of killing him during the storm. Loupe settles the matter by asking Dr. Han to perform an autopsy, assuring the businessman that if there is any evidence of foul play, he will be compensated appropriately. When the doctor confirms the man's cause of death, however, he can't explain what he finds.

There is no additional gunshot wound. He wasn't strangled. There isn't any bruising on the corpse. Dr. Han wonders if it was a heart attack that did him in. That is, until he cuts him open. His lungs are flooded with seawater despite not a drop of water found around the corpse.

There are murmurings about a curse among the fisherman, and Habernathy, superstitious fellow that he apparently is, affirms that, if that be the case, Carrow got what he deserved:

Drowned above water, cursed by the sea for his lusts.

8

Fish Out of Water

5 Weeks Later - 2nd Day in the Month of Light - New Chernobyl Bay

IT IS A JOYOUS TIME TO BE A PIRATE. With the hexen and the human+ at war on every front, there is so much room for a third, untethered party to sneak in and steal as much spoil as they can. Leon and his crew find riches in the destruction left behind. When magic and science clash, the resulting calamity can be quite profitable for the right people. Technomancer-grade technologies are left for the vultures, and they fetch a high price on the black market. Wild-magic-saturated lands and seas give rise to natural fonts of magic-rich plants and sea life—people love this kind of stuff; they say it can cure disease, inspire temporary powers, and even banish La Santa Muerte herself from your doorstep.

The weeks following the storm find Leon and Thale joined "near the hip" according to Izacc who gags comically every time they walk out on deck together. Leon doesn't give a fuck. Leon has zero motivation to keep his hands to himself. Why should he when Thale is so willing, so eager, and so goddamn beautiful when he comes undone?

Dawn is just starting to peek in through the portholes when Leon wakes from a night spent in intimate embrace. Thale sleeps on, curled into his side.

Leon's quarters, which have effectively become their quarters, are in their usual disarray with a few new additions. On his workbench are his wood sculptures; an unfinished one of a sea turtle lies next to his carving knife waiting to be picked back up. Not far from them is Thale's sketchbook, the charcoal sitting on top. Thale's netted sack hangs from a peg in the wall, next to Leon's coat and boots. Leon's sword rests on the floor atop Thale's discarded hanfu, left haphazard as they were too excited to dive into each other's bodies the night before to care where the items landed.

Leon blinks slowly, sighing into Thale's skin as he untangles himself from the other's embrace. The evidence of last night's forays has grown itchy on their bodies, so Leon rolls himself out of bed. He returns with a dampened washcloth, which he runs across Thale's torso. Thale giggles at the treatment, batting away Leon's hands.

"So cruel, waking me like this!"

"We should have cleaned up before we went to sleep," Leon persists, straddling the wriggling Thale to finish cleaning his skin.

"Then you shouldn't have exhausted me so."

The towel goes flying as Thale pushes Leon over to nuzzle into his throat, biting down on the smooth skin there. Leon lets his eyes slide shut as Thale touches him, caressing the muscles of his pecs and abdominals and trailing over his biceps and forearms before pulling Leon's right hand up to his mouth. He tongues each digit, kisses Leon's knuckles, and drags his teeth across Leon's palm.

This is something he has come to notice over the last week or so, the amount of attention Thale pays whenever he is touching Leon. It strikes Leon how intent Thale is outside of making love. Just days ago, Thale massaged his way from Leon's feet all the way to his hips. The whole process took an hour, Thale's hands tracing over every muscle, every divot, every nook, and cranny of Leon's legs and feet as though he had never touched such limbs himself. His fingers skated over the knobs and bolts of his mechanical parts, never shying from the more than human parts of him, like he was examining a cache of gemstones. The ministrations left Leon feeling as jointless as did any orgasm.

Thale's love for his hands was another matter entirely. So extreme at times that Leon feels envious toward them, but then he chides himself and wonders how it is possible to be jealous of his own body parts. They are his after all.

"Why do you like my hands so much?"

"I like all of you, Leo."

Leon sighs dreamily as Thale presses two kisses to his hand, first to his pulse point and second to the slot that allows him to hook into a mainframe, and he remembers another Thale from before they started this journey, wrapping a handkerchief around his hand and telling him that his hands were precious.

"Yes, but you especially like my hands."

Leon can't see Thale's smile, but he can feel it where it presses against the back of his hand.

"They're powerful and gentle and expressive. They make beautiful things in appreciation for the things you've seen and experienced. They tell your story. I love the way they touch me like I'm something to be treasured. So, yes, they are pretty precious to me because they are the song of your humanity."

He delivers one last kiss to a sword callous at the base of Leon's index finger. He seems to contemplate something for a moment, turning Leon's hand over and over.

"Hey, Leon, can I show you something later?"

Leon blinks.

"Sure. What is it?"

"Well, you've been trying to get me to go swimming with you for days."

"But we are shipping out today. You'd rather go swimming in deep water? You realize there are sharks in deep water, right?"

Thale opens his mouth to answer but is cut off by a sound Leon really should've expected to show up soon.

"Mrrrow!!"

Coconut jumps onto Leon's cot with a yowl. How she manages such a feat with such short legs, Leon doesn't understand but manage it she does, landing on Leon's feet and pawing insistently at Thale's over the sheet with a continuous stream of meows and loud purrs. As good as any rooster, Coconut is always timely in requesting breakfast. It isn't a bad thing. It keeps Thale's schedule because if Coconut is begging for food, it is also about the time for Thale to begin his tasks in the galley, prepping the crew's breakfast.

Leon groans as Thale rises from the bed. Leon watches with half-lidded eyes as the man bends to collect his garments from the floor, first the orange tunic that barely covers his ass, then the black and red overrobe that reaches to his ankles. He pads around collecting this and that, Coconut nearly tripping him twice as she winds through his legs, before reaching back over to give Leon a peck on the lips.

"Don't pout. Haven't you had enough of me?" he teases at Leon.

Leon smirks, leaning against the pillows. "Never."

"Brat. You'll see me at breakfast.

"Too long from now. Besides, most everybody else is still at port. It's just us and Loupe onboard right now. You'll be getting up to cook for two people."

Thale shakes his head.

"Well, those two people are fed for the morning."

Leon sighs, acquiescing that he is going to lose this round. Getting Thale to flub his responsibilities is nigh impossible.

"I better see you eat this morning! You never eat with the crew."

"You know I always eat while I'm cooking."

"Do I though?"

"I tell you I do, don't I? And I'm not exactly wasting away either," he says, turning to exit the room.

"No, but I want to know what you ate."

"Of course, Leon. Whatever you want, Monsieur De Mares."

He offers a sarcastic bow to Leon and then disappears, the tail of his robe flicking out behind him as the cat follows him out. Leon's eyes trace Thale from top to bottom, lingering over the swell of Thale's succulent derriere until it is completely out of sight.

Leon falls back into the cot with a huff.

Coconut is being fussy again. They've been out of port for nearly five hours, and she's been running around the deck, chasing after Cassiopeia's loose bootstrap for the last thirty minutes. They are well out to sea, the wind blowing in their favor, and Thale is currently in the galley cleaning up after the crew's scattered lunch schedule.

"*Mrrow*," she mews up at Leon while he whittles the final details on that sea turtle.

"Do I look like your dad?"

"*Brrp...*"

"If you're hungry, go find Thale. He can feed you."

Coconut rolls over, making a cute, close-eyed expression at him. She bats at the air in front of her, and he has to remind himself that it is a trap.

"*Mrrew.*"

Leon's shoulders sag, and he sets aside his knife and sculpture. Since her feline majesty can't seem to fend for herself, he'll have to find Thale for her. He scoops the cat up by her armpits, holding the animal in front of him like a doll. She licks her nose at him and stares him down, making a *mmrf* sound as her hind legs kick at nothing.

"Oof, Leon's daughter needs his attention again," snickers Yoshi.

"She is not my daughter."

"Right, she's Thale's. That makes her yours as well, doesn't it?"

Touché.

"You need a better hat, Guadaloupe."

Loupe looks up from where he is currently trying to mend the ripped up old tricorn he stole off of their old ship before they started sailing on their own. The thing is more torn fiber than actual hat at this point, and the feathers that once adorned it are more like sticks hanging out at odd angles.

"As opposed to you who doesn't even bother with much more than a scarf over his head. Have you no care for your eyes, Lee?"

"My eyes are just fine."

"Really, because we were worried there for a second," shouts Cassiopeia from the bowsprit.

"Nah, he's only blind when Thale is around," cackles Yoshi. "Though how you managed to still beat that Ericson fellow at knucklebones is beyond me. You weren't even looking at the dang jacks."

"Jealous, Yoyo?"

"Hell no. That kind of talent can make me money at port."

"Except he doesn't bother going into port anymore, does he?" sneers Izacc. "Can't blame 'im though. Even I can understand the appeal of cabining-in with Thale."

"You sure you're straight, Izacc?" asks Cassiopeia.

"For Thale, I don't think any man has the capacity to be completely straight. I'd gladly bat for Leon's team if that meant I got to experience the full force of that peach."

Leon punches Izacc in the side. "Get bent, Izacc!"

The lycan howls with laughter while bending a piece of metal between his grimy paws.

Thale finds him at the aft later. He sidles up next to him at the railing, looking out at the sea calmly rolling underneath a clear blue sky. Leon has finally finished carving the dang sea turtle. It's sitting on his work bench in his quarters. He'll show Thale later once they turn in for the night. It's his best wood carving yet.

"You know for such a '*vato*,' you're very patient with small animals."

Coconut, apparently, needed to be picked up and ferried down into the galley like a spoiled princess just so she could curl up in her basket for an afternoon nap.

"Eh, she's just lucky I like her papa."

Thale rolls his eyes.

"I don't know. You enjoyed petting her once she settled in your lap. You even made her purr."

Leon shrugs, turning around to meet Thale's gaze. "Gotta get approval from my step-daughter."

"Is that all?"

"Yes," he quips.

"Liar."

"Still a pirate, you know. It's a prerequisite."

There is a small uproar from across the deck as the fishermen once again haul in an empty net.

"I have never seen such a group of incompetent fishermen. No wonder they needed to contract a pirate ship. No fishing company in the world would hire them."

"It's not their fault."

"Oh, then whose fault is it?"

Thale shrugs.

Leon shakes his head.

"So, what is this thing you're going to show me later? Should I be looking forward to it?" He gives him a lecherous grin.

Thale pushes him away by the face. "Gross, Lee. It's nothing like that. It's to do with where I'm from."

He sounds nervous. Leon frowns. He has no reason to be nervous.

"Thale, you do realize that whatever you choose to tell me about your past won't make me change my mind about you. You could be the son of a king or the bastard of a prostitute for all I care. You'll still be mine."

Thale laughs. "Well, I'm neither of those things. My parents were what you would call artisans of a sort."

"Were?" asks Leon.

Thale looks down at the water, a sad smile on his lips. "They died in an accident a few years back. I kind of set off on my own after that."

"Mmm," replies Leon. "My pa was a fisherman. He died at sea when a pirate ship sank our boat. The only reason I'm not dead too is because they thought I'd make a good cabin boy."

"And your mum?"

"Back home, I guess. It's not like I've been to visit."

"Would you ever want to?"

Leon scoffs as he turns his back to the ocean leaning both elbows on the rail.

"I doubt she'd be happy to know her boy turned into a pirate."

"I think she'd be happy to know her boy is alive."

Leon just shakes his head.

Thale's fingertips brush under his chin as he coaxes him to turn his head toward the taller man. "We could go back one day. If you ever wanted to. Home is a place you can always return to."

Leon puts on his best shit-eating grin and reaches up to catch Thale around the shoulders.

"Why would I need to do that when my home is right here?"

He presses Thale bodily against the railing, hips grinding together.

"Leon De Mares!"

Leon crowds in close, smiling wide and mischievous up at the man.

"Quick, douse 'em before they start snogging again."

Sea water splashes over them, drenching both Leon and Thale from head to foot. Yoshi and Izacc are positively rolling on the floor in their laughter, a pair of buckets on the floor next to them while Cassiopeia and Loupe look on from across deck. Thale slips clean out of Leon's hold and falls to the deck with a pained groan. The saltwater gets in Leon's eyes, and he screws them shut as he rounds on his crewmates, not noticing the sound of ripping fabric behind him.

"What the hell, you guys! Are you fucking kidding me! Just because—"

"Leon." Loupe's voice is so severe, Leon immediately ceases his rant. That's when he notices that Yoshi and Izacc aren't laughing anymore, and everyone's expression reads shock and, most notable in the pale lines of their faces, fear.

"Wha—"

"Leon, get away from there." Loupe's voice rises in near panic, a decibel Leon has only ever heard once before, and it was just before Leon took a bullet to the shoulder.

"What?"

"I said get away from him—now!"

Him?

That's when Leon finally notices the pair of crimson fins dipped in the most vibrant shade of red Leon has ever seen twitching at his feet. He follows the fin up, a long tail of at least six feet in a deep dark burgundy and shimmering black and orange in the sunlight and scales that shine so bright, they seem to be dipped in gold. The valleys and ridges of the tail frame sharp hip bones, hips that just the night before Leon had left searing bruises over during their love-making. The hem of Thale's now torn undershirt hides any more scales or skin from Leon's analysis. He finds Thale's face, somehow even more ethereal with his black hair hanging wet around his face and the script-like patterns around his eyebrows and cheekbones that glow despite the bright sunlight.

"Leon." Thale's voice is different, but the same, richer but muted as though it isn't designed to transmit sound through dry air. "Leon, please. I can explain."

Leon doesn't need an explanation. The truth is staring him in the face. Thale. His Thale is a merman, a siren, a rényú.

Leon recoils. The delicate hands that have touched him countless times are now webbed and tipped with sharp keratin claws.

How is this possible?

"I knew there was something off about you." Habernathy's cane taps against the wood of the deck as he paces forward, his men flanking him. "No human is that beautiful, and your voice is otherworldly. Who would have thought that I would find my prize on the very ship I contracted for my fishing trip?"

Leon turns, understanding what this man has been looking for all this time.

"You've been fishing for mermaids."

"Yes, though a merman will do as well. Thank you, son, for making my task so easy. Smith, get the net."

Habernathy's new right-hand, Smith, steps forward with a fishing net in hand.

"Thale, get out of here!"

Leon shouts as Cassiopeia and Izacc grab him and pull him away from Thale who is hissing and snarling at the hulking man heading his way. Thale takes off on his hands, practically flinging himself toward the ship's rail despite the remnants of his clothing still hanging around him in tatters, as effective as any net in impeding his movement. He claws his way out of them and tips himself over the edge to go overboard, but without legs and a whole half of his body useless out of water, he is too slow. The net falls over Thale's head and torso. A harsh yank pulls him back onto the deck.

Leon struggles against Cassi and a now wolfed-out Izacc as Thale fights the net, tangling himself farther in its trap. The spiny ridges at his back and elbows catch between the squares. The dorsal fin becomes so tightly wound in it, Leon can see blood starting to ooze from where the netting cuts into Thale's scales.

"Let me go!"

Yoshi is in front of him then.

"Leon, you're not thinking clearly. He'd as soon kill you as kiss you."

"Yoshi," Leon growls.

"Get a hook in that tail. Hoist him up."

The order comes from one of the cronies and another steps forward to follow through. Thale lashes out with his tail, striking the sailor across the face. There is a sickening crack, and the man's dead weight drops to the floor.

"Fuck! Hold 'im down."

It takes two of them to hold Thale still enough, and the merman gives an inhuman shriek as they stab the hook into the meat of his tail, then yank him into the air like a fishing trophy.

Despite everything happening to him, Thale sings. It is not the same sweet dulcet tones he's heard Thale sing for him and the crew since he came aboard the *C-Devil*, nor is it the same otherworldly music Leon has heard on the horizon. It's harsher, edged with anger and fear, and the resulting phenomenon is unlike anything Leon has ever seen.

The sound pierces over the entire area, and every man on board is forced to slap their hands over their ears. Even Leon is forced to his knees as pain spikes in his head. The puddles of water on deck vibrate, and the waves surrounding the ship rise high enough to splash over the rail.

"Somebody get a muzzle on that thing!"

Several men are quick to respond to that, pulling rope and leather while one of them circles his hands around Thale's head. Thale opens his mouth wide to reveal a row of sharp fangs and hisses. The man draws his fingertips back before the merman can snap his jaws down on those fat digits. The sound of a whip snaps, and Thale shrieks as it strikes him across his tail.

"No," whispers Leon as the muzzle is secured, and the furious crescendo of sound comes to an abrupt end. Leon wilts. Izacc's supernatural grip on his arms returns, the intention of the hold shifting from restraint to something more akin to support. The lycan mumbles something in his ear, but Leon can't process the words. It's unimportant.

He wants someone to punch him, slap him—hell! shoot him if they have to—anything to make him wake up from this nightmare. Anything to turn the day backward, so he can nudge Thale awake again, nest himself between the older man's legs, and sink into the feeling of being whole again for the first time in forever.

Instead Thale is in front of him, hung upside down by his fishtail while a greedy aristocrat titters in delight, a heavily ringed hand reaching through the netting to touch Thale's face.

"You are going to make me so much money."

He draws his hand back when Thale shakes himself violently, his eyes dilated above the gag and muzzle preventing him from using his last means of defense.

"Feisty one, aren't you? That's good. People will pay to see something that fights back. Tell me: are the legends true? Do your tears turn to pearls as they fall?"

Predictably, Thale doesn't answer, glaring daggers at the aristocrat.

"How's Ericson?"

"Dead, boss. That thing broke his neck in one blow."

"Dr. Han, your advice?"

The old man shuffles his way forward, pressing his glasses up his face. He examines Thale like a scientist studying his latest sample.

"He's stronger than he looks. And he apparently has the ability to control water with his voice. I can't wait to get some samples once we're settled."

"That certainly explains how my dear cousin somehow drowned above water," he says, looking at Thale like he is Aztec gold. "How he must have offended you to risk exposing yourself like that, and yet it was a seemingly harmless prank that brought your little secret to light."

"Sir, I worry that he may still get loose in his current state of being. It would be impractical to try and transport a creature like this fully intact."

"Hm, and how do we solve that problem?" Habernathy's eyes glint before he turns to his assistant. "Chop the tail off."

Smith steps forward with an ax, the blade aimed toward Thale's tied fin. Leon shakes off the hands holding him and lunges forward. The ax comes down on Leon's sheathed sword, the blade of the ax mere inches from Leon's face.

"You won't touch him!"

Smith, despite being taller and broader than Leon, struggles to force the ax down. Leon swings his right leg and kicks the man in the gut hard enough to send him windmilling backward. Habernathy frowns.

"I know you were *close* with him before, but don't be a fool! He is less human than your hexen crewmates."

"We're human, too, ya dirtbag," growls Yoshi.

"That's debatable." The man ignores the witch's ire, leveling Leon with a long-suffering look. "He's no different from the tuna you had for lunch today, boy."

Leon sees red.

"He's human enough for me." Leon unsheathes his blade and draws his pistol. "You are not chopping off his tail. Not unless you want to lose one of your own limbs."

The man laughs at his threat. "The poor boy is delusional. Too long under the merman's enchantment to know fantasy from reality."

Smith moves toward Leon, ax rising.

"Perhaps we should put him out of his misery."

"Now, hold on," Loupe steps forward, a hand on his pistol. "Nobody does anything without my say so."

Habernathy draws a gun and points it straight at Loupe.

"Do be reasonable, captain. This is your payload. Do you really want to risk losing it because one of yours was too much of a lovestruck fancy to see reason?"

Several things happen at once. Leon's mates draw their weapons and step to encircle him and Thale. Habernathy's cronies all have their weapons drawn as well, swords and pistols pointed at Leon's crew.

"Leon is a member of my crew. You can have the merman, but you and your cronies are guests here, and while I would rather not have a firefight on my own ship, I will not hesitate to shoot you for harming one of mine. Then we can all end up dead and none the richer for it."

Habernathy presses a button on the tip of his cane.

"The Cetoic Trading Company thanks you for your hospitality."

Leon's eyes widen as, from out of the newly arrived barrels, a cluster of moving clockworks surface. Five fully armed sea bots (humanoid, amphibious automatons made for oceanic battle) line the deck, ready to annihilate anyone on their master's command.

"I fucking hate synthetics," Izacc curses.

The CTC or Cetoic Trading Company are the most widely known group of slavers in Deus. Scorned by those in and out of power, the only ones who sanction their dirty business are the masters they supply bodies to. Leon is about to cock the hammer on his pistol when Loupe sets his hand on Leon's forearm.

"You'll have to forgive our subterfuge. My cousin's death, disturbing as it was, made me realize I was closer to achieving my goal than I have ever been before. If only I'd realized how close. We could have ended this whole thing weeks ago. But nevertheless, you have my thanks, Captain Cortez."

"So, you repay us by staging a mutiny?" Loupe's voice sounds pinched, like he is holding himself back from murder.

"It's only a mutiny if you fight against it, *jefe*." The spanish title comes out mocking, mispronounced to sound like "Je-fii." Habernathy holsters his gun. "Now, I am not a total scallywag, Captain. I am quite indebted to your crew. I would hate to have to shoot any of you. Especially this young man who saved my life during that storm a few weeks ago. So, what do you propose? How can we reasonably sort this out so that everyone gets a favorable outcome?"

Loupe jerks his chin in the direction of the standing glass tank.

"You may not believe what I do but to maim a person of the deep is to offend the very ocean itself, and I'm not about to risk having my ship sunk for your greed. You brought that fish tank onboard for a reason. Fill it up and keep *el náyade* in there. Should keep him secured until we reach your destination, don't ya think? After that, I want the second half of the money you promised us, you and your men gone, and the promise we'll never hear from you again."

"I accept these terms," says Habernathy, tucking his hands into his pockets. "On one condition."

"What's that?" snarls Izacc.

Habernathy points at Leon. "I want him locked up. He's too heavily influenced by the siren's call. I don't trust him to act rationally."

Leon opens his mouth to protest, but Loupe beats him to it.

"Done."

"Loupe!"

"Shut up and do as I say, Leon."

Leon's knuckles itch to punch the sneer off of Habernathy's face as he claps his hands and offers a faux bow to Loupe. His form is all wrong.

"Then we have a deal, Captain. Alright, you heard the man. Get that tank filled and get the goods in for storage. In just a few days, we'll all be the richest bastards this side of the Cetoic Ocean."

It doesn't take as long as Leon feels it should. But tank filled, Thale is lowered in through the top hatch, still tangled in the netting. He is grateful when Yoshi hops onto the top of the tank with a dagger to cut the tangled ropes away. Thale sees the blade and tenses.

"Easy, easy. I'm not gonna hurt you," consoles the witch. He doesn't know if Thale actually decides to trust the witch or if Yoshi is using his psionic suggestion, but the merman eventually settles enough for him to safely cut away the ropes. As soon as the net is cut away, the lackey holding the rope pulley lets go, dropping Thale, hook, line, and sinker, into the tank. Smith slams the hatch shut, and a padlock is latched around the hinge lock. A key makes its way into Habernathy's hand and then around his neck on a steel chain.

"I'll be keeping this, Captain. I'm sure I also don't have to tell you that my sea bots will be keeping a guard over the tank for the remainder of our journey. You understand. It's not that we don't trust you, but..."

"Never trust a pirate."

"Exactly."

"You'd make a good one yourself if you weren't a back-stabbing merchant."

"I'll take that as a compliment, sir. You know, my client is a Seraphim navalman. The country is amassing as much offensive power as they can muster right now. They're even open to hexen aid. I could put your crew in for a recommendation, if you'd like."

Leon doesn't pay much attention to the exchange as he drifts toward the glass tank. Thale has floated up from the bottom and braced his hands against the glass, eyes wide in fear. The muzzle over his mouth and nose prevent Leon from seeing his face.

Leon lifts one hand and settles it on the glass over Thale's own palm.

"I'm so sorry," he whispers, and he wonders if Thale can hear him because his shoulders sag. Thale startles as a towel hits the glass ("Haha! Give us a kiss, sweetheart!"), and he backs away from Leon, sinking down until he is settled at the bottom of the tank, curled in on himself like a shrimp.

Cassiopeia and Izacc come up on either side of him, catching him around the shoulders.

"Come on, Leon. You can't be near him. Gotta get your head cleared."

"My head is clear, Iz."

Izacc just shakes his head sadly.

Leon notices, helplessly, the slight shimmer of a gemstone forming at the corner of Thale's eye before Cassi tugs him along, ushering him toward the cells.

I will get you out of there, Thale. I promise it on my life.

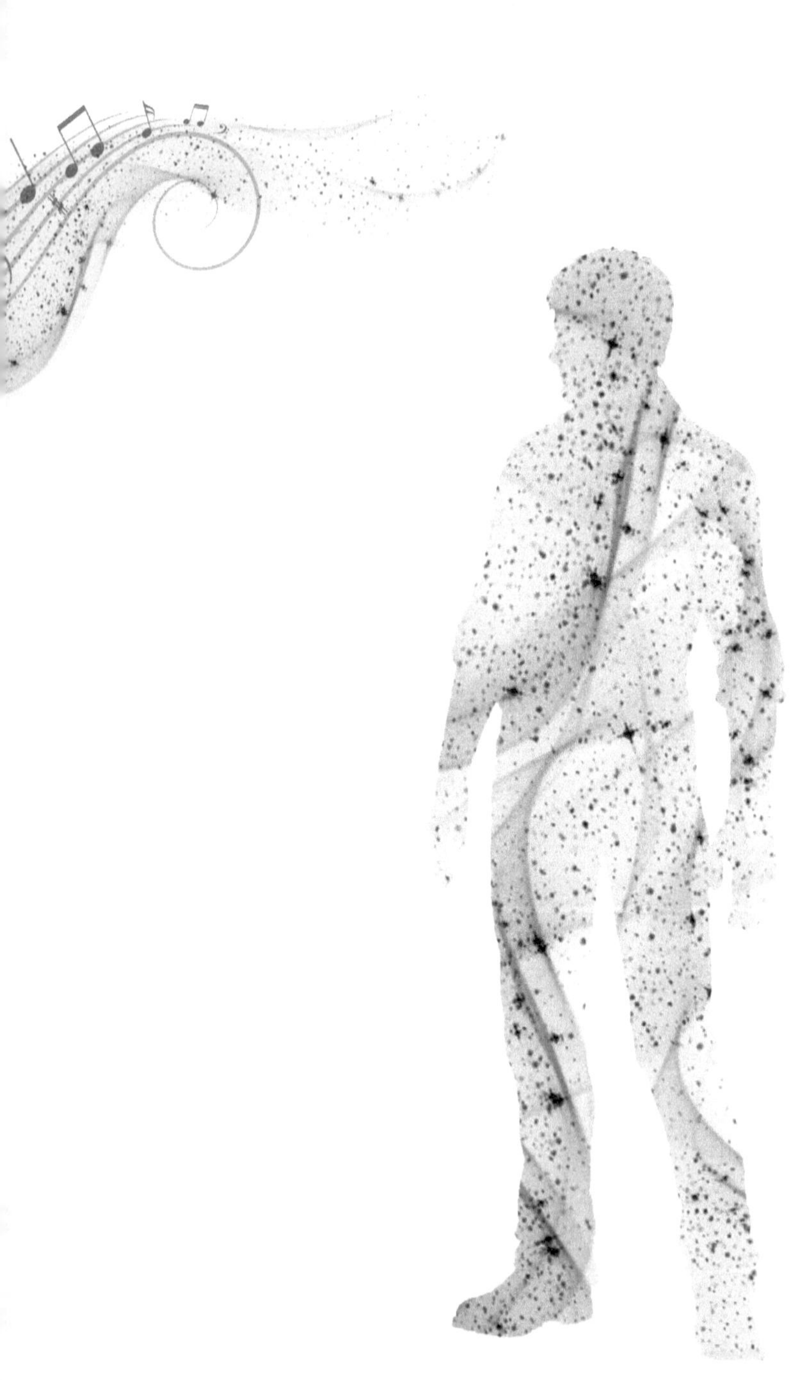

9

Roll, Boys, Roll!

LEON FIGHTS AGAINST HIS CREWMATES the whole way to the cells, kicking and growling at them like a wild animal. He even bites Cassiopeia's forearm as the woman is shoving him into the cell.

"Merde, Leon! Have you lost your damn mind!"

Leon lands in a topple on the hard ground. The shackles chained to the wall rattle as he slams against them.

"He just found out he's been fucking a fish. I'd go a bit looney in the head, too." Izacc's tone is pitying.

"He's not a fish," snarls Leon.

"Well, he ain't human, either," answers Cassiopeia. "Lords below, I can't believe we've had a merman onboard this whole time. We're lucky we aren't all dead."

"That's enough, you two."

Izacc and Cassiopeia go quiet as Loupe storms into the brig, keys at the ready to lock him into the cell. When the lock clicks, Leon kicks the steel bars.

"Loupe, you know this is wrong!"

Loupe gives a nod to the other two. "Tell Yoshi to start on supper. I don't want anyone down here without my say."

The pair leave without a second glance at Leon. So much the better. Leon doesn't want to see the pity in their gazes again.

"Loupe!"

"I'm sorry, Leon. I should have done better."

"Then let me out. I can fix it myself. I'll rescue Thale and—"

"It isn't human, Leon!" Leon flinches from the ferocity with which Loupe shouts at him. "And you're damn lucky it didn't drown you like Carrow."

"Carrow deserved what he got. Thale is not a cold-blooded killer."

"And how would you know that?"

"I just do."

"Look, we were all taken by its charms, and for that, I'm sorry. I should have been more vigilant. I should have protected you better."

Leon gnashes his teeth. "Have you forgotten about the breach that was repaired during the storm?"

"For all you know it called that storm!"

"Stop calling him an 'it'!" shouts Leon, punching the bars.

"Everything you thought you knew about that creature is a lie, Leo. It lied its way onto this ship, and it lied its way into your bed."

Loupe kicks a nearby bucket of mop water. The wood clatters across the floorboards before crashing against the far wall.

"I think he was going to tell me the truth."

"You think it was going to tell you the truth," Loupe parrots, wringing his own face. "Wake up, Leon! You've been played!"

Leon grits his teeth, jaw set in a stubborn line. Loupe sighs, lighting a lantern for Leon.

"Cool your heels, Leonito. It's better this way. You can sober up. Then when we reach port, we can put this whole thing behind us."

"Loupe..."

The older man pauses at the doorway.

"I know you hate mermaids because of your father, but it's Thale. You played craps with him the other day. He helped you brace your wrist after you sprained it at the helm. He started adding avocado to your dinner when you told him how much you liked it. He isn't a monster. He's Thale."

Loupe doesn't respond. He just storms away.

Leon drifts with the waves, not much more to do than sleep in the darkness of the brig. Drift and remember the flash of red scales under the water, of a mouth sealing itself over his and breathing oxygen into his burning lungs. How utterly stupid could he be to not have realized the similarity between that urgently given kiss of life and Thale's fond, love-soaked kisses given on dry land, between the sheets and the folds of the night, equally urgent but for something else entirely.

He dreams of mermaid tears and sea song and wonders if he is burning with fever or with despair. Memories of being ten years old and gentle arms winding around him to keep him from being taken by the tide and hurled headfirst into the rocky reef. Was that Thale, too? Was such a thing even remotely probable?

The matching tears certainly tell that story.

When he doesn't dream, he paces, a pent-up tiger in a cage, itching for freedom and action. Time is measured by the bland meals that are brought to him by unfamiliar faces speaking in tongues he doesn't care to understand. He ponders over curses and love songs and tries to remember when and if he ever felt Thale's magic touch him. He ponders over fingers curling around a head wound at the back of his skull, of the gentle threading of those fingers over the area and the utter feeling of surrender that stemmed from the treatment. He also remembers being pulled back from it like cold water being thrown over his head, and he knows without a shadow of a doubt that Thale never sought to put him under a spell. And with this knowledge, he also knows that he will devote himself to this ardor for the rest of his life because to do otherwise would be to succumb to death's embrace.

No enchantment could fabricate the flame that was lit in his very soul the moment he met Thale. No measure of separation will ever douse that flame either.

"I lament that we are back to Yoshi's piss poor cooking. It's been two days and already my tastebuds have died"

"Fuck off, Cassi."

Lucidity returns to Leon at the sound of his crewmates' voices nearing. He frowns in confusion. He thought Loupe banned them from coming down here.

"That's how you speak to a lady, Yoshi?"

"What lady? I only see you."

A fist hits flesh, then laughter, followed by a tray of food sliding through the cell bars. He isn't hungry.

"Eat up, buttercup. You'll need your strength."

Ha! Whatever for? So I can sit here yellowing in my own piss and sweat?

"Leave me alone."

Leon rolls over and puts his back to them, closing his eyes and praying they'll just fuck off already. Unless they're here to let him out, he doesn't care to socialize. He can hear them whispering with each other, knows he is being talked about, and appreciates their presence even less for it.

"Your fish is dying, Leon," says Yoshi at length.

Leon turns his head.

"What?"

"The merman. I mean, Thale. I think he's dying. I don't know. He hasn't moved much all day today."

Yoshi looks downcast in the lantern light. Like he too finds this whole situation as unbelievable as Leon does. Cassiopeia and Izacc wear equally severe expressions.

"He hasn't been eating either," adds Cassiopeia. "The fish they've thrown in the tank with him just swim about like happy little guppies."

Leon scrambles up and over to the bars, gripping them in hand.

"You have to let me out. Let me out so I can save him."

"But what if Loupe is right and you are under his spell? What if he drowns you after you help him?"

"I'm not under a spell, Izacc, and if Thale wanted to drown me, he wouldn't have needed to come on land to do it."

"What do you mean?"

Leon would have followed his voice into the darkest depths of the ocean if Thale had willed it. It's a frightening thought, but he quells it with the knowledge that Thale would never have called him to his death. Not in a million years. But this isn't what he tells them.

"Do you remember when I went overboard? When we were attacked by that Derivan ship."

"Yeah." They nod collectively.

"I think Thale saved my life that day."

"Seriously?" asks Izacc. "You think he's been around that long?"

Leon doesn't know what he thinks. "You said it yourself. I was under the water for over an hour. I don't have lung augmentations. How else can you explain that?"

The three share a look.

"I thought I told you three to stay away from here."

"Cap'n!"

"Loupe!"

Three heads snap around and stand at attention. Leon would find it comical the way they about-face if the situation were different.

"Get out, all of you, and don't let me catch you down here again."

"Aye, sir!"

"Yes, mom."

Cassiopeia punches Yoshi as the three of them hurry out of the room.

"Come back down to lecture me?"

Loupe sighs, looking ten years older than his actual 30. "Leon, I know you think you're in love with that thing—"

"Him," snaps Leon. "Thale is not a thing, Loupe."

Loupe concedes the point. "Fine, him. I know you think you're in love with him, but it's just a spell. An enchantment. He's lulled you into feeling things that aren't real. That's what they do. They seduce sailors into the deep to drown them. It's how my father died, lured into the deep by a pretty voice and empty promises. They are soulless monsters, Leon. Cursed to live loveless lives for all eternity."

"I am not under a spell."

The man opens his mouth to speak, but Leon cuts him off. "I know my mind, and I know what Thale is capable of. Whether you believe that or not, I don't care. He may not be human, but he is still a person. He is a person with hopes and dreams and fears, and he doesn't deserve to live the rest of his life in a fishbowl."

Loupe deflates at that.

"Leon..."

"Do you know what he told me back when I was still avoiding him? Before I finally admitted that I loved him?"

Loupe makes an exasperated sound.

"No, I don't know what he told you, but I have a feeling I'm about to find out."

"He told me that the thing he fears more than anything else in the world is losing his freedom. It's as good as a death sentence for him. If what you believe is true, that he really is incapable of love, that he doesn't have a soul, that he doesn't feel anything other than bloodlust, then why has he been walking around on land? Do you really think that a person cursed to live without love would risk their own freedom just to fuck around with a human? Why would he risk everything he has just to be with me if he didn't love me?"

Loupe sets his hands on his hips and shakes his head.

"I don't know, Leon. I don't know, but there is something I do know."

"What's that?"

In all the time he has known Loupe, he has never wanted to punch the man more than when he hears the answer that falls from his captain's mouth. It leaves him cold and angry, fighting back the sting of tears in his eyes because he's right. Loupe looks at him for a long moment. He says something that Leon doesn't catch, and then leaves. When he realizes that Loupe left the key to his cell sitting atop a nearby barrel, he doesn't think further on it.

He has more pressing things to do.

Yoshi meets him just outside the brig, a finger over his lips and Leon's weapons in hand.

"What's happening?" whispers Leon as he takes the offered weapons.

"We're taking back our ship. You," Yoshi tosses a key at Leon, "are rescuing your fish."

Leon smiles, tucking the key into his coat pocket, and draws his blade. Together, Leon and Yoshi make quick work of the two men sleeping in the crew's quarters, slitting their throats in their sleep. It is as the last one gurgles his last breath that the first gunshot fires above deck. The pair race up the ladders to the main deck. Leon jumps out as the man in the crow's nest tumbles down, landing with a splash in the ocean.

"Go get Thale. We've got these bots in the bag."

Leon doesn't need to be told twice, rushing over to the tank. Leon dodges as the first robot fires at him, but he closes the distance and his sword blade slides into the cabling at the back of the machine's receptors. With the spurt of an electrical shortage, it topples over dead, and Leon takes the clear path to the tank.

The reality of the siren's condition is so much worse than what Cassi and Yoshi said.

Thale lays unmoving at the bottom of the glass tank, curled up into himself much the way Leon last saw him. What is disturbing is the gray casting to his skin and the complete lack of color in his fins. Once vibrant scarlet scales have darkened to a depressed sooty gray, the little color left no more than a dusty pink that barely radiates in the darkness of the night. Leon can't even make out the movement of his chest as he breathes, too shallow, too choked in the still water of that tank.

Leon crouches down and sets a hand on the glass.

"*Mon haut*. Thale," he calls to no response. *Gods!* Thale, who on two legs stood taller than Leon and is even longer in his true form, looks tiny, lying lifeless in the tank.

He swallows and jolts up, climbing his way to the top of the tank and digging the key out of his coat. He all but throws the padlock overboard, swinging the hatch open. He shucks his boots off, takes a deep breath, and dives into the tank. Thale barely stirs as he gathers the merman into his arms, rocking him slightly as he lifts him up and out. He sets Thale's torso against the lip of the hatch top as he pulls himself out of the tank, turning immediately to tug Thale the rest of the way up.

Thale is not light, but he isn't heavy either, Leon thinks, hooking the merman's arms around his neck and lifting his lower body into his arms. He jumps from the top of the tank and immediately kneels, cradling Thale against his chest.

"Thale, come on. Wake up. Open your eyes, please."

Thale remains limp, the barest flutter of breath on his lips.

Cassiopeia scuffles by, sword locked with the cutlass of one of the trading company's robots. Their scuffle upends a bucket of water that splashes over the base of Thale's tail. The fin twitches, and a bit of color returns to it, the scales almost lighting up in comparison to the rest of Thale's body even if they lack the full coloration they had before.

Water, thinks Leon. *He needs to go into the water. Real flowing water, not a stagnant fish tank where oxygen can't circulate.*

Leon works quickly, carefully extracting the hook embedded in Thale's tail before enfolding Thale into his arms again. He turns and shouts to Loupe who is a few feet from him fighting off a pair of ruffians.

"Loupe, get the shoreboat!"

"Leon, what are you doing!?"

He stumbles a bit as he makes his way to the railing, Thale's tail dragging on the ground like a heavy curtain. He braces Thale's hip on the rail as he turns the beauty's face toward him. He presses his forehead against Thale's, clammy and cold as ice.

"Please, let this work," he breathes as he adjusts Thale in his arms, lining up their torsos.

Leon tilts the both of them over the rail and into the freezing waters of the Cetoic Ocean. Hitting the surface is a shock to even his system. He holds firm to Thale as the current pushes and pulls around them. He leans forward and presses his lips over the still despondent merman's.

Come on, Thale! Wake up! Swim for me, mon haut. *Swim for me.*

Leon exhales all of the air in his lungs into Thale's mouth and still stays below the surface, eyes open, waiting for the twitch of a fin, the batting of an eye, the rise of a chest, anything that tells him Thale is going to be alright, but before anything can happen, he is yanked up by the collar of his coat so roughly, he loses his hold on Thale.

"No!" he yells as Thale's body drifts away into the deep.

His head breaks the surface, and he is manhandled onto the shoreboat.

"Loupe, goddamnit. I—"

A pistol cocks right next to his head. "Where's my merman, brat? What did you do with him?"

Habernathy glares down at him from the middle of the shoreboat, two of his men on either side. They must've hijacked the boat to escape the *C-Devil*. Leon lifts his hands, backing away toward the bow of the small boat.

"He's gone. Swam away."

Habernathy scoffs. "Somehow I doubt that. That fish was in no state to be swimming anywhere anytime soon. Smith, keep that harpoon at arms. You see anything move in the water, you fish it out, you understand me? I'm not losing that moneymaker. Jorgen, tie his hands. We'll need him as bait."

Jorgen, an ugly fellow with metal for a skull and a mechanical leg, binds his hands with rope and shoves him into the railing. Leon, uncaring about the treatment, keeps his eyes on the water, the image of Thale's too-still body sinking into the deep fresh on his mind.

"Want me to toss him back in the water, boss? There are some steel chains we could weigh him down with. He'll never see the light of day again."

"No," says Habernathy, scanning the dark water. "We need him. So long as he's here, the merman will come for him. It is only a matter of time."

"He won't come," spits Leon. "You killed him the moment you put him in that tank."

"Well, I suppose we will find out soon, won't we? Jorgen, bleed him."

Leon hisses as a knife digs into the flesh of his wrists. He is then lifted up and halfway thrown over the rail of the small boat so that his tied arms hang overboard. The rail digs harshly into the sensitive flesh below his armpits, and Jorgen's booted foot stomps down on his chest hard enough to make his sternum pop. His knuckles skim the water, and the blood drips down into the sea. The water splashes up, stinging into fresh wounds.

"He won't come."

"Then I'll just have to enjoy watching a shark bite your arms off."

While Leon was being trussed up and bled, the other mate, Smith, kept skimming the water, harpoon in one hand and a flashlight in the other to see as far beyond the boat as possible.

"Boss?"

"What is it, Smith?"

"There's something in the water."

"There are a lot of things in the water, Smith. It's the sodding ocean. Stay focused."

"But boss—"

Something large splashes beyond the light of the torch. Both Habernathy and Jorgen move away from Leon, hoping to find what they are looking for. Another splash and this time Leon catches a glimpse of a fin breaching the surface. It isn't Thale's though. It's the wrong color, yet the mermaid hunters don't seem to realize this.

"Ready that harpoon. Jorgen, get the net. We are not letting him get away this time."

Behind him, something tugs at the rope around his hands. He chances a glance back, and his heart stops. A pair of webbed hands are peeking up out of the water. Sharpened nails shred the rope to tatters. Those hands wind around his slashed wrists. There is a warm sensation, like his blood being stirred as the wounds heal, cauterized from within. The hands disappear, but Leon stays where he is, acting as though nothing has changed. His sword is by his feet, but three against one are not good odds. He doesn't know about the other two, but Habernathy is packing. He'd be shot dead before he could do much more than stand.

He continues to plot how he is going to get out of this situation when suddenly gooseflesh prickles over his skin as a haunting song drifts over the boat like a shroud, resonant and echoing from beneath the waves.

What will we do with a drunken monger?
What will we do with a drunken monger?
What will we do with a drunken monger
Early in the morning?

Way Hay and up he rises
Way Hay and up he rises
Way Hay and up he rises
Early in the morning

The rewritten sea shanty is sung in an eerie key, filled with dissonant rises and falls and far too slow to be anything but a death march. Smith, harpoon raised, begins to fret over the voice.

"We shouldn't be out here, boss. This is his territory. We best leave while we can."

"And go where—back to the ship? We bag this fish, and we make our way back to shore. We're as good as done for without it."

"But sir..."

"It's just some bloody singing, sailor. Leave it well enough alone. It can't hurt you."

They continue to argue, unaware of their third wheel Jorgen beginning to lean over the railing of the ship.

"Hey, gents..."

Leave him in the bed with a lusty harlot
Leave him in the bed with a lusty harlot
Leave him in the bed with a lusty harlot
Early in the morning

Rid him of the posies in his pocket
Rid him of the posies in his pocket
Rid him of the posies in his pocket
Early in the morning

Way Hay and up he rises
Way Hay and up he rises
Way Hay and up he rises
Early in the morning

A bright red glow originates from below the water's surface, a menacing contrast against the black of the sea around it. It hovers underneath the boat keel. Jorgen's nose is nearly level with the water by the time Habernathy notices something amiss.

"Jorgen, get away from the water."

"But it's soo..."

Take him for a tumble in cold waters
Take him for a tumble in cold waters
Take him for a tumble in cold waters
Early in the morning

Drag him to the deep and stow him under
Drag him to the deep and stow him under
Drag him to the deep and stow him under
Early in the morning.

Way Hay and up he rises
Way Hay and up he rises
Way Hay and up he rises

Early to his last sleep.

The song ends, and nothing happens. The virulent red glow drifts away into the darkness, and there is no further stirring beneath the surface of the water. Collectively, all three men heave a sigh of relief as though they were expecting something to happen.

"Hmm, I thought—Argh!"

A pair of hands surge up out of the water, grip Jorgen around the head, and pull him out of the boat and into the water. The man disappears below the dark surface with a loud splash. Habernathy reels backward, dropping his pistol in shock, while Smith throws the harpoon into the sea with a curse.

Leon bounds up, collects his sword, and drives it straight through Smith's ribcage. When Leon draws his sword back out, the man plummets into the water, fodder for the sharks. Leon rounds on Habernathy, now scrambling to regain his laser from the floor of the boat. The man gets his grip on it and aims at Leon, point blank range. He revs the current, but an inky tar-like substance, spat from somewhere behind Leon, blinds him before he can fire. He screams in pain, flailing and rocking the boat so violently in his frenzy that Leon worries he is going to capsize them.

Leon swipes his blade forward and across the fat man's throat, and the silence that follows is a balm to Leon's nerves. Habernathy falls sideways into the bottom of the boat, and Leon has to kick and shove to roll the man over the edge and into the water. He floats for a moment before sinking down with a release of air bubbles.

Everything goes quiet for a moment, the bubbles from Habernathy's corpse the last sound among the gentle wash of waves and wind. It is terribly dark despite the first peek of dawn just starting to lighten the horizon. Leon feels chilled to the bone, still soaked from the water.

His ears perk up at the sound of something moving in the water. There is a splashing sound and a few thuds on the far side of the boat. A dim glow warms the space around the small boat, and Leon turns to find Thale hanging from the rail of the boat, only his upper body visible above the waves. His color has returned, eyes bright in the starlight, and he is as devastatingly beautiful as Leon has ever seen him, seawater dripping from his hair and skin, down the line of his throat, over the arch of his shoulders and across the firm planes of his chest. In the darkness, the markings around his face—swirling patterns like that of the various coral Leon has seen in his life, spirals and arches and clean crisp lines that seem to accent the already perfectly sculpted bone structure beneath—glow a soothing orange rather than the fierce red they were a moment ago when Thale dragged Smith below the water.

"Hi," he says. There's an entire song trapped in that single word.

Leon swallows. "Hi."

Thale's seashell necklace tinkles as he shakes his hair of water. He quirks one side of his mouth up, closing his eyes in quarter moons as he reaches a hand up toward Leon.

"You, uh, want to help me up?"

Leon shifts toward him, setting his feet against the boards as he takes Thale by the wrists. Leon allows himself to feel Thale's pulse, notes that his skin is warm once more, no longer cold and clammy. He wonders idly if the merman runs several degrees hotter than he does. The touch sears into the pads of his fingers. Leon takes a deep breath, relishing in this, the knowledge that Thale is alive and well and will be just fine, but then he throws his weight forward with a heave.

Surprise registers on Thale's face as Leon bodily pushes him into the water.

"Leon?!" he calls as his head breaks the surface once more, face pale despite the color that has just returned to him.

"You need to leave. Leave and never come back."

"I don't understand. You—"

"Go, you fiend!" Thale recoils as though Leon has just slapped him. "You don't belong here, so just go!"

"Leon, why are you saying this? This isn't you talking."

"I don't know what fantasy you've written inside your own head, but you thought you could force me to fall in love with you; well, I don't. I don't love you. I never have!"

"Why are you lying to me?"

"I said get out of here, monster! Get lost!"

Leon throws the nearest thing to him, a broken wood bench from Habernathy's previous thrashing, into the water almost close enough to hit Thale. The projectile gets the message across, and Thale takes off backward with a flick of his tail fin. As the surface settles, Leon screws his eyes shut. His teeth clench so hard his jaw aches.

Leon waits, standing in the small shoreboat to see if he comes back. He waits so long the sun greets him. Dawn breaks over the horizon. Still, he waits. The sun climbs higher until the heat of high noon beats down on the back of his neck. He waits as the sun begins its descent. He waits until twilight streaks over the water. And finally... Finally as the sun begins to set once more, he picks up an oar, remembering his last conversation with Loupe.

"Why has he been walking around on land, putting himself at risk just to be with me?"

"I don't know, Leon. I don't know, but there is something I do know."

"What's that?"

"When this is over, you need to make him leave. You need to tell him to get lost and never come back."

"No," growls Leon. "I won't do that."

"You have to, Leon, otherwise rescuing him will be for nothing. There will be others. Greedy bastards who want to get their hands on an easy dollar, and so long as he is around you, he will be an easy target for them. If you want to truly save him, you need to give him up."

Roll, Boys, Roll!

Leon grips the oar handle so hard, blood wells around his palms at the remembered conversation had in the darkness of the brig. He steels his heart and rows back to the *C-Devil*, the sunset at his back an array of dusky oranges and reds reminiscent of a certain merman's tail fin.

Thale, in all that time Leon held vigil, never came back.

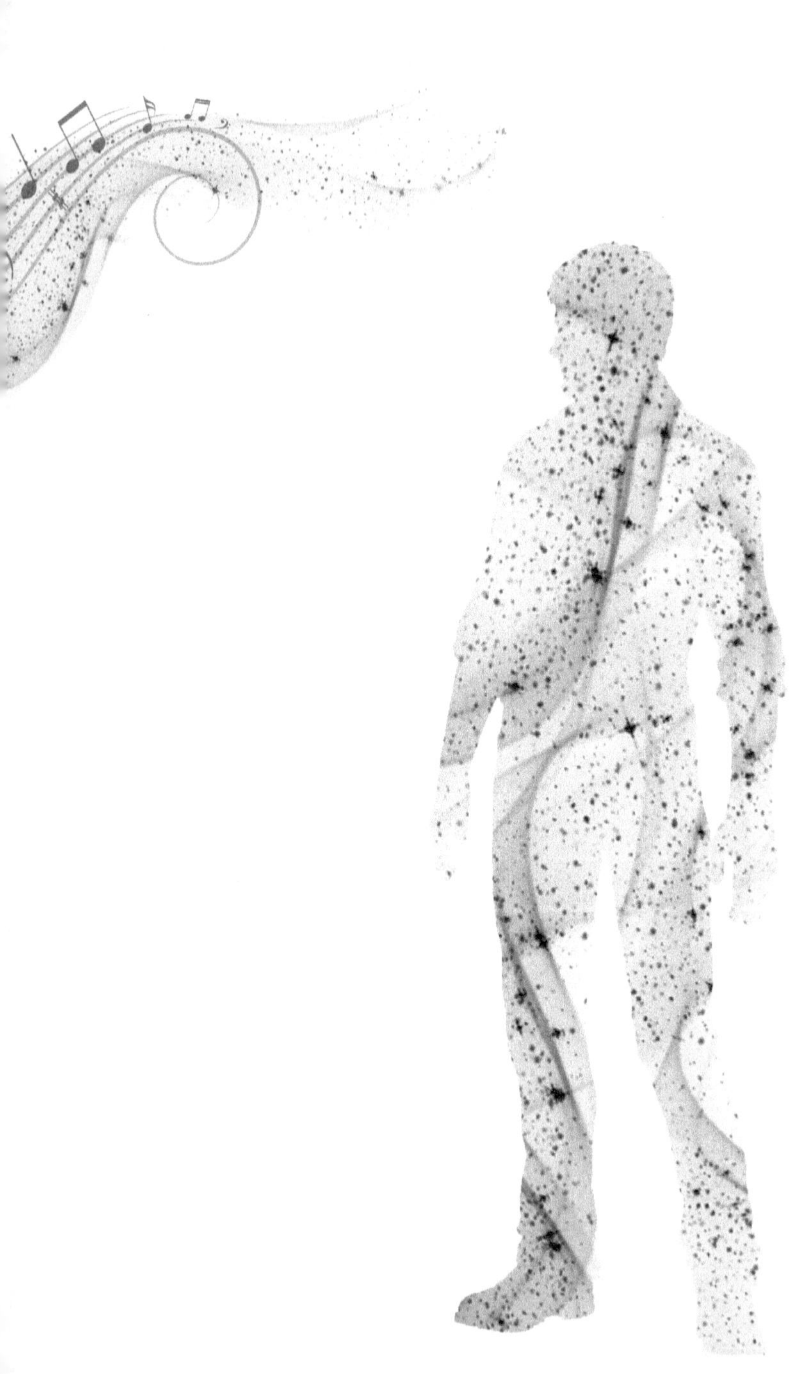

10

The Parting Glass

Of all the comrades that e'er I've had
they're sorry for my going away
and all the sweethearts that e'er I had
they'd wish me one more day to stay
but since it fell into my lot
that I should rise and you should not
I'll gently rise and I'll softly call
goodnight and joy be to you all

A verse from *"The Parting Glass"*
An Old World Hymn

Two Weeks Later - 17th Day in the Month of Light

C-DEVIL LEAVES DR. HAN, THE ONLY surviving member of Cetoic Trading Company on their ship, stranded on an island, trussed up, and surrounded by the damning evidence of his illegal association with pirates. Izacc even has the bright idea of branding the man with the letter "P" in a mockery for the man's dalliance into piracy. It's the least that could have been done to him, especially after Leon finds out that in the short time Thale had been held in that tank, he'd already started conducting experiments on the merman, but that's neither here nor there.

There is clean up to be done. Scourging away the evidence of the PTC having ever been aboard. The robots they pawn, personal belongings are abandoned, weapons added to their own artillery.

Cassiopeia unearths a small pouch amongst Habernathy's belongings that contains a colorful array of the same sparkling pearls Thale traded for his passage aboard. Mermaid tears, each of them different in color, shape, and size: blues, greens, whites, and golds. There are but a handful of them, but it is evidence enough that Habernathy has been looking to fish a mermaid out of the sea for himself for a long, long time.

It makes even Loupe storm up for a while.

The tank, wretched thing that it is, is dismantled and left abandoned at the next dock for someone else to clean up. When Loupe finds Leon later the same day, he thrusts a small pouch into Leon's hand.

"These are yours," he announces blandly before leaving Leon alone once more.

He doesn't pay it much respect at first, minding his knife as he carves out a rough outline of the tail on his latest sculpture, but when he does get to it, he almost regrets having bothered. Leon opens the pouch and pours the contents out into his palm. Sixteen identical black iridescent pearls flaked in ruby red sparkles.

Thale's tears, found at the bottom of the tank.

Weeks pass without any sign of the merman, and life returns to how it was before Thale sang for him, the same arrangement of play fights, hard work, plundering gold, and fighting the patriarchy (Cassi's words, not his.). Leon and his crewmates return to the simple life of sailing the seven seas without a care in the world as though nothing has changed other than the ridiculous sum of gold currently sitting in their hull from the mermaid tears Loupe sold at port. Everything is just as it was before.

Except...

Nothing is the same.

Not for Leon.

He has known love, has felt it in the marrow of his bones and the pit of his soul. He has ached for it, yearned for it to come back, but knows that can never be, so he resents it. His fingers itch to peel it out from under his skin but thinks he will suffocate to death without it. He wonders if this is actually why the legends say to love the sea is to love death. No mortal man could survive feeling that kind of love and having it ripped away from them. Perhaps mermaids drown their lovers, not by dragging them into the deep but by leaving them alone in the shallows, too human to follow their hearts and unable to breathe in a world devoid of the colors that burst forth in deference to their all-consuming passions. Leon certainly thinks it might be best to turn himself into the sea's hands and pray that when the water floods his lungs, he will die in the arms of the person he loves most.

But then he remembers. Thale wanted to stay. It was Leon who chased him off.

It's why he makes the decision to use Thale's tears to buy his own ship: a small vessel he can manage on his own with a handsomely sized cabin and enough space for him to sail across the ocean with little trouble.

"Are sure you want to go off on your own, Leon?"

Leon looks up from where he's tying off a pulley at the main mast to see Loupe standing at the head of the gangplank. Arms crossed and a piece of wheatgrass between his teeth, Leon's captain is the picture of a concerned older brother. Leon would think Loupe was any other sailor were it not for the pistol at his belt and his new tricorn hat complete with long fluffy feathers and beaded good luck charms.

"Nice hat."

Loupe laughs as he reaches up and pulls the accessory off his head.

"Thanks. One of my mates said I needed a new one, but I don't think this one quite suits me."

Leon squints at Loupe as the man fiddles with the brim of the hat, fingers stroking over the feathers even.

"You get on well enough," Leon declares, turning his attention back to his work.

"Mm. I suppose that's your usual way of saying goodbye. You don't."

"I need time, Lou. It's... It's too difficult."

"And I suppose carving out that new sculpture is supposed to help?" asks Loupe, gesturing to where Leon's work in progress sits next to his carving knife. It's a rough piece, still mostly unfinished. The tail still needs detailing, and the torso is a soddy imitation of the source material, but he'll get it there.

"Leave it alone."

Loupe, never one to pay much mind to Leon's tempers, strides over to the little wood carving. He doesn't pick up or touch it, but he does hum in appreciation of it.

"It'll be a nice piece when it's finished. Our Leon is ever astute in his attention to detail."

"Hn," is the only reply Leon graces him with. Loupe sighs, stuffing one hand in his pockets.

"You really did love him, didn't you?"

Leon's smile is bittersweet at best. Yoshi told him not two days ago that these things were always better to think back on from the perspective of that old adage: better to have loved and lost than never to have loved at all. Leon thinks it's utter bullshit.

"Does it matter?"

Loupe tuts. "You made the right decision. He would never have been safe around you. Around us. Around humans. Why do you think all of the fae went into hiding after the hexen fell from power?"

It was true enough. After the League took power, the unseen folk scattered to the four winds. If the witches and their ilk were no longer able to give them safe haven, they knew better than to associate with the human+. Magic and technology are ever adversarial, no matter the source of said magic. Yet, here he is a cyborg who fell in love with a mermaid.

"Guadeloupe." He articulates each syllable of the man's name in an attempt to stave off the question he knows is coming, but...

"Are you going to look for him?"

"No," Leon says with such finality that Loupe actually flinches.

"Why not?"

"It's a big ocean. Even if I did try to find him, I doubt I would succeed." It comes out snippy and short, the way he used to talk when he was still a teenager who didn't know any better. He's doing it again, taking out his frustrations on someone who is basically family, and isn't that the whole reason why he's decided to set out on his own. Leon sighs. "There is someone else I need to find first."

Loupe nods in understanding. "You know you'll always have a family with us."

Coconut pads her way across the deck with a little *brrp*. Leon holds his hand out, and she nudges her whole head into his palm, nuzzling into him the same way she used to nuzzle into Thale. It had taken some time, but she's finally warmed up to him. Not that she has much choice, mind you. She's not much of a ratter, and without Thale around to dote on her, she needs to butter up somebody for her meals, and that somebody ended up being Leon who had been the closest with Thale and, therefore, the most reasonable shift in attention, which was why she was now here with him on *The Sea Lion* rather than still on the *C-Devil*.

"*Gracias, compadre.*"

And he is surprised to find he truly is grateful.

"*Je t'en prie, Leonito.*"

To know that he has a place to return to when he needs, if he needs, is a greater gift than anything else Loupe could have given him. It is as he is mulling that over that Loupe throws the hat at Leon. He barely catches it.

"What?"

Loupe gives him a lopsided grin. "You're your own captain now, Leonito, and every captain needs a proper hat."

Loupe makes his way toward him, plucks the hat from Leon's hands, and plops it on his head without much ceremony, and for a moment, Leon is thirteen years old again, half an orphan far away from home with no hope to ever return. Loupe is the same ship hand who dried his tears, took him under his wing, and taught him how to survive until he could stand on his own two feet in this cruel world they found themselves in.

He doesn't say goodbye to his crew. Not really. Hugs are given, promises made, and well wishes delivered, but it's not goodbye. Not really. He knows he'll see them again whether it be in ten weeks, ten months, or ten years. He'll see them again.

Leon sails toward the past. For the first time in nearly ten years, Leon sets foot on the docks he used to chase his father down as a child. It is the middle of the day, and there are fishermen, merchants, and traders all along the pier. They are friendly and don't pay much mind to his attire. He even recognizes a few of them. Ladies who used to look after him on the water, an old man who once showed him how to set a fishing hook, a woman who once set aside the tastiest coconut milk sweets for him. Everything looks so much like he remembers, and his heart aches because of it.

A few of them recognize him. That in and of itself causes enough of a stir Leon wonders if he should have covered his face. Well, at least it helps direct him to where he needs to go.

The old cottage is still there. Nearly unchanged, the same sunflower patch, the same rickety fence, even the same shingles over the windows, albeit certainly in need of repair. Maybe he can take care of that later. He can oil the fence, tend the garden, and repave the walkway. He can do all of those things. He has time.

He knocks on the door, worrying at his lip as he waits. When no answer comes, he knocks once more before he loses his nerve. The seconds stretch by, and when still no answer comes, he decides to call it and try again another day.

Leon retreats so rapidly, he almost misses the soft call of an older woman's voice.

"Hello?"

He freezes, sweat beginning to bud at the back of his neck. He lifts a hand to his hat, realizes his hands are shaking. He must not have moved for a long time because the woman at the door makes a sound of irritation.

"Can I help you, young man?"

Leon turns slowly, clearing his throat and letting the hat on his head fall to his side so that his face is clearly visible. There is a crashing sound, but he doesn't meet her eye. His throat is still clogged with emotion when he speaks.

"Bonjour, Mama..."

Leon sets his eyes on his mother for the first time since that fateful day. She had fussed over him incessantly, making sure his collar was right, and his boots were well oiled. She is older, of course, wrinkles lining her face and hands, her hands which were just a moment ago carrying a potted plant. She also is much shorter than him which is probably also a given considering how much taller he is now then when he was 13.

"Le-Leon?"

"Yeah, Mama. It's—It's me."

His mother takes several shaky steps onto the porch. She looks so fragile. Leon takes two long strides to reach her. His hands come to her shoulders to steady her even as her hands come up to caress his face.

"Leon. My Leon. My baby... alive..."

He nods. Her thumb brushes under his eyelid, smearing dampness across his cheekbone. He's crying. He didn't even notice. She pats him on the cheek, tugging at him, and he leans down to let her hug him fully.

"*Mes dieux!* Let me look at you."

She laughs up at him, her eyes turning to crescents as she takes him in, looking him up and down.

"You're so tall. Most handsome too."

"I'm sorry, Mother. I'm sorry that it took me so long to come home."

"Shh," she hushes him. "You're here now. That's all that matters. Come inside."

And as she pulls him in and settles him at the old dining table, a warmth he hasn't known in eons settles into his chest. Somewhere between telling her about the attack on his father's boat, becoming a pirate, his crew, and an abridged version of the PTC story, Leon's heart begins to ache a little less.

For the moment, settled in the warm creaking walls of his childhood home, he realizes that Thale was right. Home is in the people you can always return to, the people who will never judge you wanting, the people who will smile simply because you are smiling, the people who embrace your happiness as their happiness. His crew... His mother... His...

He closes his eyes and smiles at the silly questions his mother asks. Does he still prefer pepper in everything, or has he learned to appreciate other flavors? Will she ever get to meet his crewmates? Where has he been, and what were the most amazing sights? He answers her calmly, happily, helping her prepare supper in the small kitchenette.

That evening in the small seaside cabin, even as Leon tells his mother all about his life on the high seas, he doesn't tell her about Thale. He doesn't know how.

The days pass, and Leon relearns how to be a son. He fixes up the house, makes repairs, and runs errands for his mother. She, in turn, dotes on him, feeds him more food than he can stomach, and fusses over him just like she used to.

He doesn't stay with his mum, too used to the gentle rocking of being on water to sleep on solid ground. He lives and sleeps on his ship. It's comfortable for him, and somehow, insignificant as it is, the decreased distance between him and the vast open water makes it easier. He spends his days on the land, enfolding himself in distractions. Occasionally, Leon catches himself staring out to sea, caught up in the daydreams and memories of what once was and what could never be again.

"You're in love," his mother declares to him one afternoon while Leon is up on the roof repairing a leak he noticed during the last storm. "You've been staring at the ocean for nearly fifteen minutes like a lovestruck guppy."

He'd been zoned out for that long?

"Sooo," she coos as she climbs the ladder to sit with him. "Who is she, and when do I get to meet her?"

Leon shakes his head with a scoff. "It's not a girl, ma," he looks down, refusing to meet his mother's eyes, "and I don't know where he is."

Work worn hands fold around him. His mother's lips are warm at his temple.

"He must be very special to have captured my boy's heart."

She has no idea...

"Well, if it is meant to be, the stars will guide you back to each other. He'll take one look at you, and then who in their right might would ever run from my handsome boy?"

Leon shakes his head but lets his mother continue her ramblings.

Later that night, Leon lies awake in bed. Coconut's little body is curled up beside him, and where normally her weight is a reassurance, it does little for him tonight. He feels hot and itchy. Maybe it's because of what his mother said. Maybe it's because there is a full moon, and the tide is heavier than normal. Maybe it's because the ache in his chest is all the worse for no reason at all.

He huffs and rolls over.

The roof of his cabin is plain enough: dark wood, darker nails, crossbeams, and a pair of hanging lanterns. His sparse belongings are scattered throughout the cabin. His coat hangs off a hook, his boots sit by the door, and his latest sculpture, freshly completed rests atop his work bench, a pale mockery to the real thing. There are other things in the cabin that are not his own: a netted sack hung off a chair, a black hanfu that is too long for him tucked into the standing wardrobe among his spare clothing, a half-used sketchbook tucked into a corner of the worktable.

The moonlight shines in through the window, and he wonders if maybe he should open the pane. It's stuffy and warm in the cabin, so he arranges his limbs under him and rises to let the outside air in. It is a cool night. The breeze is a balm on his overheated skin. He closes his eyes and leans his head against the pane. That's better, but it does nothing to relieve the itch under his skin, like an army of sea urchins crawling just below the dermis.

There is a bottle of rum by his elbow. He's tempted for a moment to just down the whole thing, but he reaches for the water instead. He drinks long, his throat working over the cool fluid until there's none left. It does not help, and he slams the bottle down hard enough to startle Coconut awake.

The cat makes an upset sound then jumps from the bed, scurrying off into the darkness somewhere.

"Goddammit, Leon! Get a grip!"

He punches his fist into the wall, hears a satisfying pop, and does it again and again and again until he has no more energy left, and his flesh knuckles have split open around his augmentations.

"Argh!"

He screams as he collapses onto the floor in the fetal position. His hands pull at his own hair, the pain a sensation he can make sense of. It's physical. Physical is good. Physical will heal. Emotional... Emotional is another thing entirely...

It spirals and multiplies. It scabs over and then rips open over and over and over again. A never-ending cycle of wanting and losing and hoping and despairing. This juxtaposition of delight and delirium. He wants to curse Thale for doing this to him. For saving him. For loving him. For listening to him. For leaving him. He curses himself for sending him away. It was the right thing to do. It was the only thing to do. Being selfish wasn't an option then, and it isn't one now because he has nothing to be selfish about. Thale is gone. Gone, gone, gone. Lost to him among the waves and the ocean current, gone home to the deep blue abyss, and the sooner he makes peace with that, the sooner he can move on with his life.

He doesn't want to move on.

"Thale, come back," he whispers. "Please come back."

He doesn't know how long he lies there, tucked in the space between self-pity and self-hate, begging into the silence for something he will never have. If he lies here long enough, dawn will come, and then, he can chalk this whole thing up to a fever dream. A break in reality. A nightmare. He can rise with the dawn and keep moving forward like nothing is wrong, and the world isn't cruel enough to keep from him the person that makes his heart sing. In the light of day, he can hope that maybe his mother is right, and the stars will line back up for them. In the light of day, he can trick himself into believing that fate isn't laughing at him. In the light of day, he can work himself into forgetting that he is a complete and utter fool... But there are hours between now and then. Hours where hope doesn't exist, and the world takes pleasure in its own cruelty.

"*Mrrow.*"

The sad little sound accompanied by tiny little licks and nuzzles to his face pulls Leon back from a precipice he didn't realize he'd fallen into. His eyes feel swollen and wet. The floor under his head is also damp. God, he hates being a crybaby, but the cat seems to enjoy it, lapping up his salty tears while a deep rumble resonates from her chest.

"Coconut..."

His knuckles throb as he lifts his bruised and battered hand up to pet her and then thinks better of it, not wanting to smear blood all over her fur.

"*Mrow.*"

She folds herself over his face, and he doesn't have the heart to push her off. He just curls an arm around her and lets the vibration of her purr lull him back to calm, back to sanity, and down into sleep. He chuckles in the back of his throat. Like this, with her belly over his ear, he can almost pretend her purrs are more musical than they really are, and he smiles, letting the illusion wash over his senses.

Seasong echoes in his head as the rest of the world falls away.

When Leon wakes, it is still dark outside, maybe an hour or two before dawn. Coconut is no longer on his face, and the blankets have been pulled over his shoulders. *Wait...* He's in his bed. But he'd fallen asleep on the floor. He sits up, and the covers fall around his waist. He raises his hand to his face, and notices that it is wrapped in clean dark purple seaweed. When he unravels the oceanic bandage, he finds his knuckles completely healed, not even any bruising around the joints that he had so brutally battered just hours ago.

That's when he hears the song.

Are the sparkling waves enough to keep you warm?
When you think of the light that radiates from me,
Will you still let me sing for you?

Leon jolts out of bed and runs onto the deck.

Twinkle, twinkle like your body.
Hidden among a sea of lonely stars,
I can still find you.

Out here, the voice is clearer, a soft tenor that cascades over the water like sea foam. Leon jumps up on the port rail and holds onto one of the suspension lines for balance as he scans the water for a familiar shape.

There is a rock outcropping surrounding the lagoon not far from the docks, and that is where Leon spies the upright figure seated there, the glow of moonlight reflecting off of a waterfall of long black hair, the glittering scarlet of a long red tail and shimmering scales. He can almost make out the gleam of the markings he once saw frame the most beautiful face in the world.

"Thale!"

He knows he has been heard when the siren's song cuts off abruptly, and the figure dives over the rock edge back into the water. The bioluminesce of Thale's patterned markings glow through the waves.

"Thale!"

Leon doesn't hesitate. He dives headfirst into the ocean, descending all the way to the rockbed where he floats long enough to open his eyes against the sting of saltwater. Bubbles obstruct his vision, and the tide is stronger than he expected, but he stays long enough to catch a glimpse of something humanoid swimming ahead of him. He pushes off from the seabed and swims to the surface.

His head breaks through the waves, and he yells, "Thale!"

He hears a splash and swims toward it.

"Wait!"

He ducks back under the surf and swims even as the current attempts to pull him in the opposite direction. He does what someone should never do in a riptide. He fights the current, swimming headfirst against it, and he doesn't give a lick of a care. His resolve hardens as a shadow flits across his limited vision, and he surges that direction as long as he can until his lungs start to burn. He kicks toward the surface, but before he can break into the open air, a strong wave crashes over him and rolls him back under. He exhales as slowly as he can manage, moving with the roll of water before his head breaks the surface. He sucks barely half a lungful, then the tide is pulling him back under.

He is flung almost all the way to the bottom where the sand gleams white in the moonlight. He kicks off again at a diagonal rise to the surface, feeling the pounding of the surf about him. Another current catches him and pulls him back down. He tries to roll with it, and it flings him straight into the rocks he saw Thale sitting on earlier. The impact forces the air from his lungs, and he has to close a hand over his nose and mouth to prevent himself from inhaling. He grips onto the rockface and tries to haul himself up, but another wave hits him, shoving him along the outcrop. His lungs burn, and he heaves himself forward just as a pair of arms wind around his waist and haul him upward.

He lands flat on his back on the rock and inhales as much air as his greedy lungs can suck, coughing up water the whole while.

"Leon... Leon! Breathe. Please, don't die!"

A new galaxy bursts into existence at the sound of Thale's voice, that beautiful, haunting, impossible voice, and his eyes snap open to see the merman himself hovering over him, fear marring that beautiful face. In less than a heartbeat, Leon's hands capture Thale's head, pulling the merman down so he can claim the elder's lips in a searing kiss.

Leon tastes sea salt and fresh clean ocean on Thale's lips. He drinks the other down like a sinful ambrosia, life-giving and etheric. Leon's right hand trails down Thale's spine, touches the spiny ridges, finds them smooth and sleek and keeps going, stroking the thin membrane between each bony protrusion. Thale gasps, and Leon takes the opportunity to carefully slip his tongue between Thale's lips and into his mouth. When Leon does this, Thale pulls back.

"Leon, don't—"

"Shhh, shh, trust me."

Thale opens for him as Leon pries his lips apart once more, diving in, greedy for more of Thale's taste. In this form, Thale's teeth are sharp, like a cross between a shark's and an eel's, and Leon glides his tongue carefully along their ridges so that he doesn't cut himself on them before tangling his tongue with Thale's own.

All the while, Leon's hands continue to trail over Thale's body. Over the spiky protrusion at his elbows, down the front of his chest and stomach, around his waist, and finally into the curve of his hips where mammalian skin gives way to smooth scales and ridged spines and flared fins.

Thale moans as Leon fingers the silky soft line of his tail just over the curve of the man's hip bone.

High tide churns around them. Leon presses up and over to hover above Thale. Both of his hands catch around his trim waist and hold. His mouth descends from Thale's lips, trailing down over the damp skin of his neck and chest until he can nose at his pulse, feel it for himself under his cheek, relish the sound of it in his ear.

"Leon, you can't. I—" Thale sounds breathless and over-wrought as though Leon has stolen the air from his lungs. He writhes below him as Leon bites into the skin at his pectoral. At his feet, Leon feels Thale's willowy tail fins flair and sway back and forth. "You—You could've drowned. What is the matter with you? Why would you…"

Thale's voice is unsteady, puzzled through with doubt and confusion, both of which Leon has put there.

"I would rather drown in your arms this very minute than live a thousand lifetimes without you." Thale's breath hitches. "I love you, Thale. I love you. By land and by sea, I love you."

"Leon," Thale's voice is softer, so soft Leon almost can't hear him over the crashing of the waves. "I-I…You… I love you, too."

He trails off, and under Leon's hands, something truly astonishing happens. Scales give way to warm skin, the spines soften and melt into human shapes and angles, and Thale's face shifts from something otherworldly to something familiar, equally beautiful but more human. Hands that are no longer webbed reach up and wind into Leon's hair, dulled nails scratching against his scalp deliciously. When two bare human legs wrap around his waist, Leon truly knows that he has returned home.

"How is this possible?" he whispers into Thale's mouth.

Thale tilts his upper body up until their foreheads touch. His eyes shimmer in the moonlight.

"Leon, it's my love for you that allows me to walk in your world."

Joy swells like a tsunami. It floods through Leon's entire being and spills over unrestrained to Thale in the over-flowing strength of his smile. Their next kiss is wet with sea mist and emotions too strong to manifest in any other element but water. There is a slight tinkling sound on the rocks as scattered pearls bounce and roll their way into the water. Leon dries the rest of Thale's tears before they can solidify with peppered kisses and careful brushes with his thumbs.

Thale's smile forces a laugh out of him that is powerful enough to rock the both of them. Thale laughs with him, gentle and melodic above the white noise of the ocean around them.

Leon worships Thale's body with scattered kisses, bites, and love-filled caresses as though Thale were a sea god and Leon his sole devotee. His hands slide down warm flesh, lips trailing after as he makes his way down to the ridge of his lover's hips, dipping lower to kiss the merman's sex, hot and erect and already dripping with excitement.

"Leon."

The hushed call of his name is all the incentive he needs to take Thale's length in hand, lips closing around the tip to taste Thale's skin, a warm flavor reminiscent of salted caramel and toasted coconut. Thale all but sings as he takes him farther in his mouth, the fingers of his other hand already dipping down to tease Thale's entrance. The fingers of his left hand circle his rim while he suckles at Thale's cockhead. He groans, surprised to find slick already collecting there, naturally secreted by Thale's body. Gods, he cannot wait to discover more about Thale's anatomy. Leon gives one last full-bodied suck to Thale's cock before lifting up and rolling them at Thale's naked insistence if the tugs at his ears and hair are anything to go by.

Leon entered the water without a shirt so all Thale has to peel off of his body are his trousers. Leon helps him with the ties and buttons at the front, and then Thale is stripping him. The last barrier between them gone, Thale arches himself backward.

"Thale, wait. Let me—" Leon calls out in warning, but with hands braced on Leon's chest, Thale impales himself on Leon's substantial member without preparation, apparently deciding he doesn't need it. Leon's eyes roll into the back of his head, and his back arches off of the rockface at the friction.

"Thale," gasps Leon as he is enfolded into Thale's tight, damp heat, the man's body stretching around Leon's girth as a long drawn out moan falls from his open mouth. Gods, he is so tight, Leon feels like he is suffocating right up until he tilts his hips forward, drawing another loud moan from his lover. He sits up to enfold Thale in his arms. Thale tilts his head back, long hair cascading down his back and waist to brush over the top of his ass as Leon sucks on the sensitive skin of his collarbones.

They move slowly together, rocking against each other as though time were inconsequential. Seasong surrounds them, and Leon doesn't question how or why, not when the notes fall from Thale's lips like a prayer, intermingled with calls of his name as he makes love to him.

Leon slides deeper into Thale on every thrust, the friction of each slide delicious enough to make his toes curl. Leon is rewarded with tiny, pleased moans and surprised gasps whenever he rolls his hips in just the right way to catch that sensitive button deep inside the merman until he can't take it anymore. Until neither of them can take it anymore.

Thale's gentle pace gives way to a more harried tempo. Leon grasps at Thale's hips, moving him easily up and down his length as Thale's knees spread wider on either side of him.

Leon rolls them once again, Thale's back to the rock giving Leon full control over their movements. His right hand comes up to wrap around Thale's engorged length, and he drives forward in a frenzy, his hips slapping against the soft flesh of Thale's backside, all of his senses reduced to where he and Thale are connected as bolts of electricity branch out along his spine every time he sheathes himself in Thale's heat. They are so close to the edge where the rockface slides back into the water that Thale reaches up to grip the edge and pull himself closer to the water until the tips of his hair and his hands can sink into the sandy shallows of the lagoon. Leon follows him and watches in astonishment as the water inspires orange and red patterns to flow across Thale's skin, vibrant and luminous in the dark of the coming dawn.

The sight spurs him on.

Thale writhes in rapture, a portrait of ecstasy as Leon's cockhead brushes against his lover's prostate, and Thale unravels beneath him. His spine arches into a perfect bow, head tossed back so far he nearly submerges himself in the lagoon water, and the sound that spills from his lips is inhuman in its unearthly beauty, siren's song mixed with utter abandon. Thale's release spills over his fist, and the merman shudders as Leon's own orgasm rips through him, leaving him bereft of his senses, all the world fallen away except for the exquisite creature in his arms.

Thale. His Thale, whose heart beats like a drum under his ear.

Euphoria soaking like a damp cloth over his awareness, he returns to the tune of feather-like kisses along his brow and cheeks.

"Leon."

The sun is just beginning to brighten the horizon. They'll need to move soon. Once the sun touches the horizon, the beach will be bustling with activity. The seagulls are already stirring, fishing for their breakfast among the small crustaceans that have lollygagged too long in the shallows.

"Leon..."

Leon lifts his head to look into Thale's eyes. The glowing markings have disappeared back into his skin, but Leon's fingers trace over the memories of them anyway.

"Stay with me, Thale. Stay here with me." He laces their fingers together, bringing Thale's palms to his mouth. "Keep me," he whispers into the soft skin of the merman's wrist.

Thale draws himself up, hands lifting to lace into Leon's hair, and his lips are soft and coaxing as he claims Leon's mouth for his own. He pulls away far too soon to whisper into Leon's ear.

"Until the oceans dry and the land returns to the sea."

Thale smiles like the sun, bright and warm and enduring. The center of his universe.

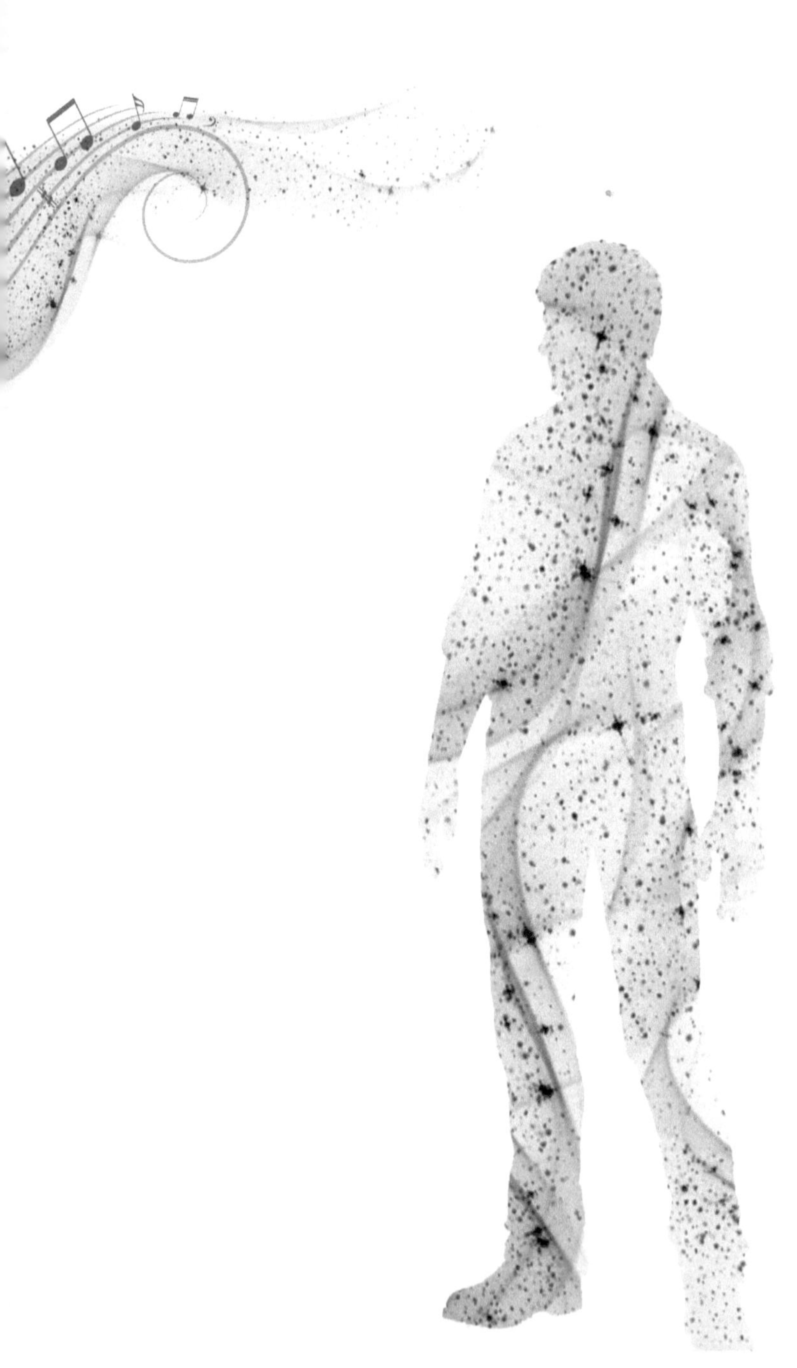

Epilogue

COCONUT HAS CAUGHT A MOUSE. A rare sight indeed, one that Leon will be sure to give her lots of rewards for later. But now that she has one, she doesn't seem to know what to do with it, tossing it around deck and batting it about before finally setting it at Leon's feet.

"Well, I don't want it."

Coconut looks up at him with wide amber eyes, lifting one paw to pat his pant leg.

"*Mrrw.*"

"You caught it. You eat it. Isn't that what you're supposed to do with your prey?"

She gives him a little chirrup and then closes her eyes, her mouth making a cute "w" shape: a picture of pride. Must have something to do with present company.

"Oh, did Coconut catch something?"

He turns as Thale walks onto the deck, as graceful on two feet as he is without in the water. When he meets Leon's eye, his face lights up in a brilliant smile. One Leon cannot help but return in kind.

"Looks like it. Now she doesn't know what to do with it."

As he speaks, Coconut darts toward Thale, twining her way between his feet. Predictably, this doesn't end well as Thale, ever stressed about maintaining balance, loses his footing and trips over her. A moment of panic crosses his face, and then he is flailing toward the floor.

Leon catches him before he hits, and they both go down laughing, landing in a sprawl with Leon's limbs akimbo and Thale's head cradled to his chest.

"I swear, I'll never get used to walking around. How do humans worry about keeping their balance all day long? It's exhausting," Thale mumbles into Leon's shirt. The tips of his ears are red. "And then you do things like run and jump and dance, and it's just impossible. No wonder you are all always covered in bruises."

Leon cards his fingers through Thale's hair, pushing it away so he can see the merman's face. "I can always find you in the water. You'll breathe for me, won't you?"

"That would be impractical for the long term."

Leon's heart flutters.

"I suppose I am cursed to be covered in bruises for the rest of your days."

"I'll help you stay on your feet."

"You'd better."

Thale's kisses are like the ocean, vast and bottomless, and Leon will bathe in them for as long as he has the good fortune to be showered in them. They break apart as Coconut yowls, apparently disgruntled about not being the center of attention. Leon helps Thale to his feet, fingers intertwined and skin warm in the sunlight of the bay. Those ocean eyes shine at him, their depths colored with warmth and life and the deepest of adorations.

He could fall into those ocean depths for the rest of his life, content and happy in their warm currents.

Leon has always loved the sea. It is vast and mysterious and holds so many beautiful things. It is gentle and ferocious, life-giving and deadly. It is everything Leon has ever wanted to know and more. Leon could never deny the depths of his love for the sea, his infatuation with its song. He has loved the sea since the day he was born. He knows this to the core of his being.

Leon smiles, broad and uninhibited, and Thale smiles right back.

He never thought, in a thousand years, the sea would one day love him back.

Indexes

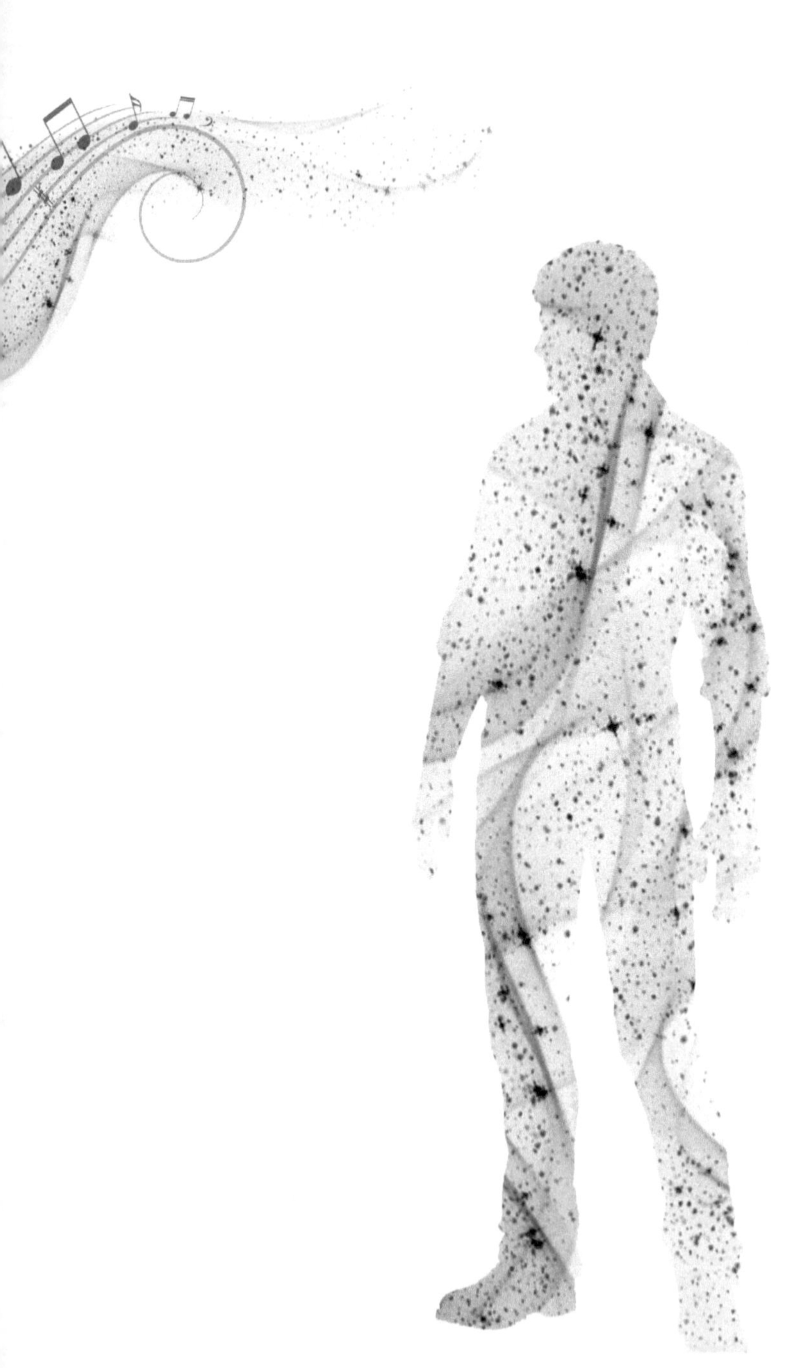

The Deus Calendar

The Thirteen Months of Deus and Their Associates Festivals

Month of Ice   Start of the New Year

Month of Frost   World Liberation Day
                        (WitchSlayer Celebration)

Month of Song   Spring Equinox

Month of Storms

Month of Planting   Human+ Festival

Month of Light   Summer Solstice

Month of Soil

Sea Song de le Corsaire

Month of Fire	Summer's End
Month of Falling	Autumn Equinox
Month of Darkness	Hexennacht (Halloween)
Month of Harvest	
Month of Cold	Firefly Hearth Festival
Month of Hearths	Midwinter Celebrations

Glossary of Terms

- Adept – An augmented person equipped with military–grade technology. Certified to hunt and track hexen.

- Corsaire - French word for Pirate - A person who lives on the outside of the law, stealing, pillaging, and raiding according to their own whims.

- Cyborg – An augmented person possessing a set minimum of technological enhancements, or a human+ possessing enhancements essential to their ability to live (i.e. respiratory life support, mechanical hearts, spinal augmentations to prevent paralysis).

- Fae - The Unseen Folk - These are the creatures of Deus who have always been. Often called fairies, these are magical creatures who are sentient but not derivative of witch magic like fairies, pixies, elves, mermaids, and centaurs.

- Hexen – The Spell Folk – Magic users and creatures reliant or resultant of witchcraft. (Examples of Hexen: Witches, Lycans, Vampyres, Goblins.)

- Human+ – A person who has permanently integrated technology into their bodies. This can be as mediocre an augmentation as a cochlear implant or as extensive as a prosthetic limb or neural net.

- Lycan - A shapeshifter of any kind, though typically lycans are known for being able to transform into wolves or wolf-like creatures depending on what branch of lycanthropy they are partial to.

- Merfolk - Mermaids and Sirens - Magical creatures of the sea, long thought to lure sailors to the deep with their sweet voices. At this point in Deus history, mermaids are difficult to come by since the hexen regime has been dismantled across much of the League. As the witches disappeared so too did the safety their spells provided, so the merfolk keep themselves scarce beneath the waves away from human contact.

- Technomancer – A League–certified human+ capable of channeling energy through their technology. Technomancers are specially trained and equipped to hunt and kill dangerous fae, hexen, undead, and other magical creatures. This also includes other human+. Their augmentations are top–of–the–line and require an immense amount of discipline to maintain and control.

- Witch – A practitioner of witchcraft, the act of molding and utilizing wild magic to effect change in the outer world. Witches in Deus achieve their powers and abilities through a mixture of blood–inheritance and practical study and are considered the most dangerous of beings as the practice of unrestricted magics can lead to psychological breakdown and magic fever.

III

Glossary of Characters

- Leon De Mares - Human+ - a pirate on the crew of the *C-Devıl*.

- Anders Thale - Our mystery beauty who meets Leon while at port. His past is a magical mystery to be discovered throughout the story.

- Guadeloupe Cortez - An unaugmented human and captain of the *C-Devıl*. Someone needs to keep a level head when dealing with cyborgs, vampyres, and witches.

- Izacc - Hexen - A lycan and crew member of the pirate ship the *C-Devıl*.

- Cassiopeia - Human+ with a mechanical leg. A pirate and demolitions expert on the crew of the *C-Devıl*.

- Yoshi - Hexen - A witch and pirate on the crew of the *C-Devıl*.

- Coconut - Thale's cat, a little munchkin who snuck onto the *C-Devil* as they were leaving Calypso City.

- Habernathy - A seemingly wealthy nobleman who commissions the crew to allow him to fish without a license. He is desperately searching for something in the waters.

- Carrow – Habernath's cousin and right hand man.

- Smith - Another of Habernathy's crew.

- Jorgen - Another of Habernathy's crew.

- Dr. Han - The doctor Habernathy brings on board. Why a group of fishermen need a doctor along on their endeavors, who knows?

Book Club Questions

1. How does Leon's character change over the course of the story?

2. How does the crew of the *C-Devil* resemble the trope of found-family?

3. If you were to travel to any beach or seaside, where would you go? How do you think that place compares to Leon's childhood home?

4. Saenz writes several sea shanties within *Song of the Sea.* One is an original while others are altered versions of well-known folk songs. How can you imagine some of your favorite songs changing one hundred, two hundred, maybe even three hundred years from now?

5. When did you figure out Thale's little secret? Do you think he is indeed the mermaid that saved Leon's life as a child?

6. *Song of the Sea* is inspired by both "The Little Mermaid" and *Pirates of the Caribbean.* What parallels

do you see between those two pieces of media and Thale and Leon's romance?

7. How does this story differ from other M/M romances you've read?

8. If you could cast any celebrity to play Thale and Leon in a movie version of *Song of the Sea,* who would you cast?

9. Do you agree with Carrow's punishment, or should he have been given a proper trial?

10. What would you do if a mermaid fell in love with you?

LYRA R. SAENZ IS A WRITER OF SCIENCE Fiction/Fantasy. A romantic at heart with a love for supernatural horror, she believes that while happy endings don't come easily, they do come, even if it means excising your ex into a glass jar.

Born and raised in South Texas, Lyra is a multicultural, eyeliner-wielding member of the LGBTQ+ community, an animal-lover, and a cynic of all things political. She presently haunts the Houston area with her amazingly supportive partner and her feline-shaped void, Violet. Lyra grew up bouncing between her Chicano and Scandinavian heritages never feeling like she really fit in one world or the other.

Despite growing up on enchiladas and lefsa, she'll never turn down an offering of sushi or pho. And while her friends were getting boyfriends and girlfriends, she was too busy crushing on dreamy anime and manhwa characters to bother with real people. So with one foot on either side of the border and her head full of East-Asian pop culture, she started creating her own worlds.

A lover of all things witchy, paranormal, and ghostly with a side of Victorian-futurism, cyberpunk, and posthumanism,

Lyra imagines worlds where the IT tech is a werewolf and the coffee machine has a fairy living inside it but the androids love to take walks down the forest trail and host the occasional bonfire. When she isn't lost somewhere between an inkwell and a notebook, she can be found acting as a throne for the real queen of the household -Her cat and her royal majesty demands snuggles constantly. Or sitting and listening to her partner play video games while she unsuccessfully knits and/or binges her latest international tv show.

LGBT Romance

AJ Buchannan

Orchestrated Love

Eskay Kabba

Hidden Love
Not So Hidden
Signs of Affection
Deeply Devoted to Him
Honest Love
A Plane and Simple Connection

Lucas LaMont

Roman's Reckoning: Type 6
Mikaél's Moment: Type 6

Stephan's Resurgence: Type 5
Anastasia's Arrival: Type 6

Stormie Skyes

Check Yes, No, or Maybe

V.C. Willis

The Prince's Priest
The Priest's Assassin
The Assassin's Saint
The Champion's Lord

Fantasy, SciFi, & Paranormal Romance

Amanda Fasciano

Waking Up Dead
Dead Vessel
The Dead Show
Dead Revelations

Beau Lake

The Beast Beside Me
The Beast Within Me
Taming the Beast: Novella
The Beast After Me
Charming the Beast
The Beast Like Me
An Eye for Emeralds

Swimming in Sapphires
Pining for Pearls

Chelsea Burton Dunn

By Moonlight
Moonbound
Bloodthirsty

D. Lambert

Rydan
Celebrant
Northlander
Esparan